I0571610

ESCAPE

FROM

INCONSEQUENCE

By

Francis Voignier

Cover design by Francis Voignier
"Looking up the Mosel Valley" 1984

Though this book is a work of fiction, it is immersed in the private experience; consequently, names have been changed to protect the privacy of living individuals. Their replacements are by no means to be confused with real people unassociated with this story.

Library of Congress Cataloging-in-Publication Data
Voignier, Francis 1954—United States
Escape from Inconsequence/Francis Voignier
ISBN-13: 978-1-7345551-7-2
ISBN-10: 1734555173

Fiction – France – Nancy – Marseille – Drugs – Child abuse – Prostitution – Police – Mafia – Corruption

francisvoignier.com
Dolosse & Writs, Eureka, California

LIST OF CONTENTS

A WORD FROM THE AUTHOR

It started with one idea and then it went elsewhere. There is a lot of data in this story that comes from personal observation, and some from direct experience. But the book shaped itself as if I had stuffed the contents of my life into a sack, shaken until things started to break and moan, and then spilled the damage onto the floor, picking at random what would be used next. I'm fairly certain it's not a novel method, but then again, it wasn't what I was trying to do.

At any rate, as in my other books, there was no structure around which to build, no notion of where the path ahead led to. There was a path at least, but it wasn't part of the story—it took me to it, rather. It's probably futile to try to explain something that shies away from the staticity of rules and methods; a blank area comes closest to a picture of it.

All that to say that the faces and places in the tale are all part of the rotation of characters and events that, in one form or another, add to a whole that resonates with my core reality. I'm not saying all is true, or that I lived to see everything in their most intimate details, only that without what I witnessed and experienced firsthand, this book could not have been written.

March 10th, 2018

1 – FER

Stefan lay awake. The cacophony of crushed steel, railroad engines, tugboat horns, and the general ill-defined loudness that filled the night had sensitized every nerve in his body. His mind was bouncing around his reality, unable to stabilize the present into a comfort zone. He could even hear the sprinkle of rust particles, spewed from the mouth of tall brick chimneys, as they descended on the tiled roof, only a few feet above his head.

It must have been half-past three. The chainsaw-like buzzing of departing mopeds intermixed with the slamming of apartment doors never lied. Soon, those returning from the night shift would be sucked in a reversed pattern—in, out; out and in—part of the predictable life rhythm only briefly interrupted by illness or death when a familiar noise would be gone.

Before long, his dad, Victor, would quietly enter the basement garage door, make his way up the steep staircase to the first floor kitchen where he would pour himself a glass of milk; and then climb another flight to the void of the bedroom. It was Sunday early morning, yet technically, it was still considered Saturday's shift in steel mill reality. On Monday, barely twenty-two hours away, the alarm clock would be ringing at half-past two instead. They called it the "short weekend," in Hell.

"Hell" was a town on the Mosel River, in Eastern France, that went by the oddly fitting name of Fer, as in iron. But as Stefan saw it, it might as well have been short for *l'enfer*, which actually meant Hell. What went around came around. The majority of its men worked at the mill, while its women lived a life of two existences: one with their husbands around, the other, without. Which didn't mean that cheating was common, but it was fair to say that it was always in the gossip, as if infidelities were integral to the inhaling and exhaling of the giant factory. After all, when one third of the men were at work, the other two were not. It was simple math teamed to human biology. As a result, elaborate scenarios arose around best friends working opposite shifts, often fueled by a visceral need to blemish characters by those who had the least reason to be informed. But to Stefan, who as most teenagers in the neighborhood had to have a bird's eye view of schedules—mostly for reasons of survival—rumors of extramarital affairs belonged to the fabricated drama of under-stimulated housewives. Proofs were in short supply, while malice wasn't.

By most standards of quaintness, Fer would have been an adequate place to live, hadn't it been for the two-mile long eyesore that flanked both banks of the river, churning molten iron and steel in a dissonant and dysrhythmic chaos, while noxious plumes of black, red, and sulfuric yellow erupted out of gigantic, erect spouts. But for those who lived and died there, the notion never came. It was what it was, a rarely reflected-upon reality with its decent amount of well-supplied stores, bakeries, and an extraordinary ratio of bars per capita. In spite of the municipal whitewash that aimed at selling the few merits of residing there, generally in terms of empty promises about a better future, Stefan saw Fer as nothing more than a road to nowhere, a place for the exploitable class to work and die without having lived. In teenager rationale, the town was an endless embarrassment, one better left unspoken when visiting the big city.

It was exactly half-past four when Victor returned from his shift. Stefan's mind was racing with incoherent thoughts that refused to be chased away. He was trapped in a body shackled to a life he had no control over, while his dreams tugged at his introverted despair in unsuccessful spurts. He was too rational to lose himself in the deceit of wishful thinking, yet his vision was crystal clear; he would one day be far away from Fer, to never return.

To be a teenager with a propensity for loving rock and roll in the late sixties meant letting your hair grow— the longer the better—like Dickie Peterson of Blue Cheer. Stefan wore his shoulder length, but Victor who was tired of the snide remarks thrown his way regarding his "delinquent and unkempt fairy of a son," had released an ultimatum: haircut by Tuesday, and short!

It was never a good idea to cross Victor, but Stefan had no choice; it was his integrity against the will of ignorance and mean-spiritedness. But Tuesday was still a long way away in youth years, and by then his father might have better fish to fry, such as protecting himself from the never-ending onslaught of his wife's fury. Stefan was well aware he was buying time on the cheap, but like everything in his life, every moment came with a copious dose of unpredictability that transmogrified into a mix of resignation and anxiety to be buried deeper and deeper within the self, a place where rebellion festered.

Tragically for Stefan, Tuesday arrived sooner than estimated. Victor was in a particularly bad mood that afternoon when he awoke from his nap.

"Hey, come here; are you fucking with me or what?!" he snapped.

Stefan barely had a chance to say *no* when a blow to his face sent him reeling backwards, down the short flight of stairs towards the entryway. He felt no pain. Tears of rage rose, but he didn't have it in him to fight his own father.

"Go ahead, keep on hitting if that's what turns you on!" he hissed instead, as he picked himself up.

Victor grabbed Stefan by the hair, dragged him up the steps, and slammed him on the tiled floor of the hall. He was foaming at the mouth; his crazed eyes looked as if they were about to pop out of his head.

"Fight, son of a bitch, make it worth my time!" he menaced with clenched teeth.

The blows and the kicks kept coming amid insults and threats.

"Look at what you make me do, motherfucker! Are you gonna do something or should I just fucking kill you?!" Victor lashed.

Clumps of hair air-lifted with each movement around Stefan's curled body. The teenager said nothing, victorious within the cocoon of private martyrdom. Screams were heard, probably from his hysterical mother. The hitting stopped. Victor went out. Stefan got up slowly and locked himself in his room. He inspected the reflection of his bruised face in the mirror; the blood oozing from his split and swollen lips ran between his teeth as he forced a smile. His scalp felt raw in places—the hair would grow back as it always did.

He thought about his dad. Love had left the picture a long time ago, but nothing came to replace it. Victor was no coward; when pushed, his violence was incontrollable. He would fight anyone, anywhere, regardless of size and strength, and he fought to the death.

Stefan left his room for the bathroom. His mom's medicine cabinet was a stoner's treasure troth, the byproduct of over-prescriptions, as she went in and out of doctor's offices, hospitals, and mental institutions. He briefly glanced at labels for dosage, poured himself a glass of water, and started downing pills by the dozen.

He returned to his room, put the live MC5 album on the turntable and lay on the bed, his guitar by his side.

He had contemplated a very different exit, one from left stage amid applause, but this time, things were different, meaning had walked out of his life with the lasts of the blows—the absurd has completely taken over. There was nonetheless one victory to be had, foreseen in Stefan's mind as a road paved with regret and sorrow.

2 – JULIA & JIMMY (Tue)

To add insult to injury, the exit door never opened for Stefan. Instead, he woke up a few hours later, parched but alive. Rather than assessing the existential void created by the failed suicide attempt, he pocketed the money for the haircut, left the house incognito with his guitar, and caught the last bus out of Fer to Nancy, the former capital of the Duchy of Lorraine, a city of roughly one hundred and ten thousand at the time.

He had no idea where to go; it was winter and dark. He roamed the cold streets, bought a sandwich with the last of the money, and sat at a lonely bench in an empty park, under the faint glow of an old streetlight.

Some of the drugs must still have been kicking, as he felt the soft urge to lie on his side, impervious to the near-freezing temperature, and oblivious to the high probability of being picked up by the cops.

When he woke up, a young black female, barely a few years older than him, was sitting by his feet at the edge of the bench. He looked at her looking at him, not fully realizing he was awake. She was neither smiling nor not. The emotional message that emanated from an undefined space between her eyes and her lips indicated she was concerned, and perhaps a bit amused.

"What's your story?" she simply asked.

Stefan sat up shaking his body as if to chase the cold away, but he didn't answer. She looked at the guitar case and back at him, weighing in the validity of her interest in the teen.

"Are you any good at it?" she probed in a tone

that betrayed her awareness that the question might also be ignored.

"I'm still learning, but I want to get real good at it some day. I'm in a band with some friends, but I'm prolly the only one who's serious about it," Stefan answered.

"Then stick with it; the world needs more music and dancing. My name's Julia, what's yours?"

"Stefan."

"You're from Nancy?"

"No, I ran away from Hell," he said, holding back the tears.

"That bad, hey? You probably need a place to crash, by the look of it?"

"I can't say I don't."

"I'm sharing a space with a musician friend; I'm sure he'll be fine if I bring you over. How old are you, by the way?"

"I just turned fifteen."

"Cool, I'll be eighteen in a couple of months. But let's go; it's getting late" Julia returned.

A lanky, bearded hippie opened the door. He barely looked at Stefan and Julia, stepping aside to let them in.

"What's up, people?" he muttered.

"Jimmy, that's Stefan, he was gonna sleep in the park," Julia explained.

"Groovy, man, but this ain't the kind of weather to sleep outside. What's the deal with the guitar and the bruises?" he asked, mildly curious about the surprise guest.

"I got beat up by my old man cuz of the hair... The

7

guitar's just an acoustic my aunt gave me as a gift."

Stefan noticed the Fender Strat leaning against the Vox AC 30 amplifier.

"Is that your rig?"

"54 Strat, it's been around. Go ahead, give it a try, but no amp; the neighbors have called the cops too many times already!"

A Revox reel to reel was playing *Soft Machine Volume Two* in the background. Stefan picked up the Fender and tried a few single lines along its sleek neck, pretending to be performing with the trio. Julia sat by his side, on one of the thick cushions strewn around the room, swinging her head back and forth, trance-like. Jimmy lit a spliff, sucking in a rapid triple-toker as if to create more room in his lungs. He passed the joint around then stood up and put on a heavy llama wool jacket.

"Got to get to work; you might still be here when I get back from my baking shift. The cops are going to be looking for you; you know that, right?" he told Stefan, almost as an afterthought.

Then he was gone.

Julia and Jimmy's pad was a medium-sized studio with a kitchen area along one of the two windowless walls. The only other rooms were the bathroom and the WC. Julia lit candles and incense, rewound the tape, and hit *play*. She wore a loose dress that exposed her small, bare breasts when she bent over. She didn't wear any panties either.

The combination of his mom's medication and the effect of the *Red Leb* hash mixed with tobacco brought Stefan to the edge of sickness. His head was spinning, but he refrained from letting Julia know, mostly out of pride. She couldn't help notice his discomfort, torn between wanting to help and wishing to enjoy the high of the smoke privately. She opted to meditate out of consideration for the both of them. Stefan fell into a comatose sleep. Julia turned the lights off, save for one candle; she then lay close to his exhausted and aching body.

The morning announced itself loud and early. The high-revving of the garbage truck engine amid the banging of metal cans in the courtyard, shook the shelves in the studio. The operators, in the spirit of sharing heightened versions of the shallowness of their lives, shouted over the noise, zealous to ascertain every resident along their route was properly awakened. Stefan likened the commotion to another item from the gallery of the absurd. Julia looked at him, grunted, and went back to sleep.

It was nine o'clock when Jimmy returned with the smell of freshly baked bread and a carton of milk.

"Hey man, come and get it while it's still warm!" he exclaimed, as Stefan stepped out of the water closet. "I enjoy breakfast before going to sleep," he added, laughing.

Julia joined in, yawning, while sloppily spreading butter and jam on a split length of bread. They poured hot milk in bowls over instant coffee, alternatively dunking *tartines* in the brew and lifting the containers to their lips. The warmth of both humans and food brought a rare wave of joy to Stefan's tortured heart. In spite of the apprehension around his very uncertain future, he felt liberated from his past. He had broken the chain, even if freedom was to be measured and savored a brief moment at a time.

Jimmy excused himself. He joked that his night was ready to spread under the sun; a graphic allegory that amused the guest. He soon was buried in a pile of blankets, pillows, and comforters, oblivious to the chaotic cadence of life outside. Both Stefan and Julia privately admired and envied him—he had it all figured out.

Julia walked out of the bathroom fully naked. Stefan felt his heart jump in his chest. He thought she looked wild and beautiful.

"Are you getting a boner?" she asked, laughing.

"You may say that," he replied, short of being completely overtaken by his hormones.

"Hey, it's a shame to hide what we're born with," she pronounced, standing in front of the undraped window.

Stefan steadily settled in the reality of the moment. She was right; it was no big deal. He suddenly realized what it meant to find comfort in intimacy. Seemingly with Julia, none of it was about sex or playing head games, although it was inherently sensual and playful. Mostly, it was about daring to honor the self away from taboos, about authenticity and free-spiritedness. It was the new way. He slowly began to sense that the concept of family was a lie. There had been more family in a single night with the two strangers, than there ever was at "home" in the span of a lifetime. He returned his glance to the naked sight.

Julia was foraging for something to wear. She finally settled for an elaborate outfit that included wool stockings.

"Us two are going out; we need to get to people who can help you. Some of my friends from the university are well connected," she announced.

"Why are you doing that?" Stefan asked.

"I ran away from an orphanage in Marseille when I was fourteen, after one of the nuns whipped me senseless for resisting her when she tried to finger my pussy during a so-called random hygiene inspection. I slept in many parks before I found *the others*," she explained.

"The others?"

"There are worlds within worlds."

"What d'you mean?"

"You don't think you belong to an exclusive group, do ya?! I mean, there are thousands of abused children and adolescents, orphaned and not, that are on the loose at this very moment, in this country alone. We have ways."

"I guess I never imagined runaways could organize, but I think I see what you mean," Stefan replied, watching Julia getting dressed.

"We don't do it alone and it doesn't come for free; it all depends on how sure you are you're making the right choice. It takes a lot of abuse and desperation to get to that point," she returned, matter-of-factly.

"I heard of child trafficking though..."

"Now, you're using your brain. That's where it gets tricky with the adults. Always remember that for every beaten child, a new tormentor is never far away. For some of the runaways, abuse is like a magnet."

"Is Jimmy one of the helpers?"

"Alright, you sound like a cop, Stefan. Refrain from asking the wrong questions, they only lead to more trouble. I hope you know what I'm trying to say?"

"Sorry, I get it."

"D'you like what I'm wearing, cuz I can put something else on?" she asked, swiftly changing subjects.

"You prolly look good in anything."

"You're sweet."

"You're too nice."

For a second, Julia imagined what it would be like to make love to Stefan. She wondered if he had ever slept with anyone—probably not—but he seemed a natural around nudity. She felt at peace.

"No need to drag your guitar case around, it's in good hands here with Jimmy. Let's go!"

They stepped out onto the cobblestone courtyard. It was a brisk, sunny day. The plan was to meet with some friends of Julia's at the very popular café-bar *Le Thiers*, across the train station.

Stefan was walking on air; it felt like weeks since the time of the snafu with Victor. There were other Hells in the world besides Fer, but that day, the horizon was swollen with promise. Regardless of how hard his rational mind tried to push open the door of reality, his heart was beating in time with the tune of the moment; it went by the name of *hope*.

3 – THE OLD FOLKS (Wed)

It took a while for Victor to wrap his head around the consequences of his vicious temper, but somehow, he got the point. Funny how it went when one faced an emotional vortex.

He had expected Stefan to be back before the end of his shift, but he had erred on the side of assumption. Intense guilt suddenly gripped his guts; he knew too well he had crossed the line on too many occasions and why he had lost the trust and love of his son—a thought that often morphed into fodder for renewed rage. But without an actor at which to throw the violence, Victor had turned introvertly and was dangerously close to contemplating suicide.

Stefan's mother hadn't ceased to scream like a banshee since the commotion, accusing Victor of everything from wife-beating—which he never did—to sleeping with "all the whores in the neighborhood." The irony was that she conveniently ignored how much she also slapped the kids around, and generally for no valid reason whatsoever.

Her name was Janine, an abused kid herself. An orphan since the age of three, and a child of the state during Second World War, she never knew love, except for that time when a soldier from the invading armies picked her up, fed her real food, and told her that upon winning the war, he would return to fetch her and take her home. He most likely died on the battlefield, a lone hero in the heart of a lonesome little girl.

She married Victor, a man on the rebound, who

legally freed her from the orphanage before she got of age. And, doing so, the groom wedded a developmentally arrested child in a nineteen year old body, who, as time would tell, was about to ruin his life permanently.

It didn't take long before Janine stepped in and out of mental institutions. It appeared the town's doctor routinely scheduled her for electroshock treatment whenever she visited for whatever ailment was vaguely related to nerves. It later transpired the man was a sinister bastard who took ill-pleasure in the misery of his patients, of which Janine was a repeat favorite. Nonetheless, it was convenient for Victor to have her out of the way; so that he could do whatever Victor did when everyone's back was turned. Notably, he arranged for his daughters to be placed away, while putting his son in the care of his sister who lived a block away. But young Stefan was neither dumb nor deaf, for whatever he overheard coming from the adults who customarily ignored him, sounded like dad had relinquished his fatherly responsibilities. And thus, in the grip of deceit and disillusionment, the kids put their love in the little things that could be trusted instead: the imaginary players in a world of inert objects that suddenly inherited a beating heart. Stefan inevitably turned to a musical instrument: the lowly recorder.

Inconveniently for Victor, the state couldn't afford to pay for Janine's stay in the asylum for more than a couple of months at a time. And hence returned the incessant screaming, the threats of suicide, the hysterical dust-raising that passed for work when in truth nothing was ever accomplished, until like clockwork, she was found with her head in the oven, unconscious; or flat on the tiled floor, overdosing on prescription drugs; or bleeding in the bathtub with her wrists slit open.

Somehow, she never died, and every time, not only Victor, but the kids too, regretted that once again, she had failed at returning peace and quiet to the world. Predictably, daughters were sent off to live with strangers, while Stefan was switched from staying at the sister's house to landing with an ailing grandfather, who promptly exposed him to active tuberculosis. That year, Stefan missed most of the drama while in a sanatorium, high in the Vosges Mountains, coughing blood and being pumped with antibiotics. Victor and Janine managed to visit once in the nine month period. On that afternoon, while the threesome ate Bing cherries on the grass, a family was given one final chance to realize. It lasted for the whole of those four hours. Soon, the bus that had brought them over left in a cloud of dust. Stefan ran after it, until the faces behind the glass receded to a memory.

Victor didn't have a phone, so he had to bike the mile to the station to file a report for his missing son. He was called into the office of the lieutenant in charge and offered a chair.

"Is it his first time?" the officer inquired after finishing typing the preliminary details of the deposition, shifting his body in his chair to face Victor.

"No, but..."

"What makes it different this time around?"

"He normally returns by now," Victor replied.

"That wasn't my question. What caused him to not come back, some form of punitive method?"

"We're good to him; but he's not always giving us the respect we deserve," Victor argued.

"You're evading my inquiry. When we get your son to this office for questions, he may have a different version of the events. For everyone's sake, I advise the stories remain close to the facts. So, was he punished?"

"I ordered him to have his hair cut and he refused. Yes, we had a conflict," Victor returned.

"And by conflict, I assume it involved someone losing their temper, correct?"

"Well, we can't let them do whatever they want, can we?"

"No, we can't. So, you roughed him up, you're saying... how bad?"

"I slapped him."

"You slapped him the other times too, right?"

"I guess."

"So you must have slapped him harder this time. My take is that you beat him up pretty good, and in his mind you crossed the line. Listen, I'm no psychologist, but we deal with a lot of family matters in this department. In fact, abuse cases represent the bulk of our work. So that you know, the times of bodily punishment are over; hitting a child is a crime. We'll find your son and we'll file his story, but after that, if he's gone again, we will involve Social Services. It's a small town, Sir, and you haven't exactly lived in a vacuum—people have eyes and they talk a lot. It also happens we listen. We'll check with the relatives and let you know what we find. Good day!"

4 – LE THIERS (Wed)

Julia and Stefan joined a group at a corner table. It consisted of a couple of students, a rotation of modestly stoned musicians, and a guy in his early thirties donning a salmon-pink three-piece suit; a regular known for hopping parties and buying rounds.

"Anyone's seen José?" Julia asked after kissing a couple of friends on both cheeks.

"He was here earlier, but something came up. He said he'd be back," a Spanish musician answered.

The guy in the suit ordered drinks for everyone; Julia and Stefan settled for espressos, which bought them an easy hour's time before being bothered by the waiter.

Nancy was full of rock musicians, most of them pretty mediocre at their instruments, but they were good at posing and playing the part. Stefan was so fascinated by them that it only took fifteen minutes for him to buy his right of passage. All it required was asking the questions that showed genuine interest in their less-than-genuine stories. Gear was the big thing. Whoever owned a real Gibson or Fender over the cheap Italian models was a star; and if they happened to plug the sublime axe into a Marshall or Hiwatt stack, they were a God. All it took was well-off parents or a steady income. So, it came as no surprise that most of the "serious" musicians were high school drop-outs who worked odd jobs to feed their passion for rock & roll.

"Never mind fucking education!" one of them declared. "It's all brainwash anyway. All you end up learning is shit you don't need in real life!"

17

The students ignored him; the groups coexisted amid their fundamental differences, though generally speaking, their politics were pretty close.

In the meantime, the man in the salmon suit had made his way to Stefan.

"You like pretty girls?" he probed.

"Of course, who doesn't?"

"Want to watch my wife getting fucked?"

"Is your wife one of the pretty girls?"

"Yes, she loves being watched by young lads with hard cocks. I can take you there right now," he offered.

The proposition was unreal, but it tapped in the extreme vulnerability of budding adolescents with raging hormones. Stefan, who had just watched Julia's bare body in various provocative poses, wasn't particularly attracted to the more mature and graphic display of the flesh, pretty girls or not. He declined. Julia who had overheard, felt instantly relieved.

"Let's get the fuck outta here; we'll come back later!" she ordered, glancing in the direction of the pervert with pointed disgust.

"I told you it gets tricky with the adults. The ones we must avoid at all cost will smell a prey a mile away. I wasn't aware of that creep's story, but now I know he's into boys. It's a good thing you're smart, Stef," she said, as they walked away from *Le Thiers* in the direction of *Stanislaus Square*.

"Thanks, but how d'you know he's into boys?"

"Just the way he said 'hard cock.' Trust me on that, I'm rarely wrong," Julia replied.

"You're a lot wiser than your age, you know!"

"D'you think hanging out with a fifteen year old on the lam is a sign of wisdom?" she teased.

"A fifteen year old with a guitar and a taste for wise seventeen year olds, I think so," he laughed.

"No wonder I like you," she countered, giggling.

They got to the square just in time to converge with a students' demonstration; something to do with the mistreatment of soldiers and the incarceration of political activists in the army.

"The fuzz ain't gonna find you in here unless you do something stupid," Julia humored.

"I almost forgot about it, I guess I should worry."

"There're lots of things you should worry about; the cops ain't the worst of it. You need to make money in a hurry if you want to survive, and in your position, finding a job isn't an option. That's why the pimps love you guys. So now, pay attention; it's not too late for you to go home and make peace with your old man if he's capable of it, but if you're set, you're gonna have to learn a few tricks if you want to stay under the radar in one piece. I can help you to a point, but you'll soon have to be able to care for yourself. Ever shoplifted?"

"No."

"I was afraid of it."

"It sounds scary, though."

"The scary part was living with your dad; now isn't the time to trip all over yourself. You need a crash course and fear isn't in the equation."

"OK, I'm not afraid."

"Good! First thing: forget the small places – they're bad karma. You can't steal from those who barely survive. Make it political, or make it so that it feels like it's the right thing to do. Survival isn't a crime, it's a right. So, we do the larger places, the department stores, the supermarkets, the big book stores, the record chains... You not only need to feed and dress yourself, but you also must learn how to sell what you steal, so that you can put cash in your pocket. The cardinal rule, Stef, is that you never get greedy; greed's not just a sin, it's a fucking despicable crime against humanity. Don't ever get greedy on my watch, or I'll dump you on the spot. That's how I feel about it. Now, let's go pick something that can fit in the inside pocket of your coat—a paperback, let's say. We'll do the *Spring* department store, their book and hardware section is on the basement floor. The cashiers are at each station, no checkout lanes. All you have to watch for is the undercover guy who patrols the place. He's got curly red hair, wears a tweed suit, and pretends he's one of the shoppers. If you look suspicious, he'll sniff you on the spot and you won't be able to get rid of him; meaning that you might as well get out like a good boy who didn't find what he was looking for. So here's the plan: we go in separately, but we maintain eye contact. I'll keep watch of the guy while you find your book; at which point I'll signal whether it's clear or not. Then you make it fast and smooth, get it?"

"Am I allowed to make it fun?"

"That's the spirit, Stef; let's do it!"

Three minutes later, Julia and Stefan were back on the street, Stendhal's *Le Rouge et le Noir* snuggly tucked in an inside pocket.

"Well, that was better than expected. You'll do just fine!" Julia complimented, as she hooked her arm around his.

"Actually, it was exhilarating," he bragged.

"Make it a skill, but don't turn it into an addiction. Moderation's the key to sanity and decency. Life's a short road for those who don't respect it," she stressed.

"I was right; you're wise beyond your years."

"I don't know about you but I'm getting cold; let's go back to *Le Thiers*!" she said softly.

José never made it back. Another escapee from Franco's regime, by the name of Eduardo, informed Julia that something heavy had come down. No-one knew for sure, but one of the musicians who lived nearby heard that immigration officers had raided the place and booked a couple of guys on account of lacking proper papers.

Julia suspected the cops weren't just looking for *illegals*; most likely, they were narcs sniffing for coke and hash. José must have listened to the devil on his shoulder for that to have happened, and now he was in serious trouble. Unfortunately, he was also the main connection to the réseau, meaning things had just gotten somewhat complicated for Stefan.

"Listen, I'm gonna have to go deep in the layers to help you with this; it's going to take time too. Jimmy's cool for a few days, but he's no sugar daddy to no-one," Julia warned Stefan.

"I don't expect anyone to go out of their way for me; I can manage."

"No, you can't. You'll freeze your ass off and end up being nabbed by the cops, and if you're lucky, before your guitar gets stolen," she argued.

"Didn't you say you survived on your own before you found *the others*?"

"It was summer in the south; sleeping outside was no big deal. There were people along the way who were willing to help with food, clothes, and even cash; though I have to admit I narrowly escaped rapists on a few occasions. Each time, I had to start from scratch. But winters in the east will kill you."

"So, what you're saying is that I'm fucked?"

"Let me treat you to a hot chocolate and a sandwich; we can discuss possibilities after we feed ourselves," Julia offered.

The night had fallen behind *Le Thiers'* etched glass windows. Despite the warmth in his stomach, Stefan experienced anxiety mounting in waves. Victor's angry face popped in and out of his thoughts, making it difficult to concentrate on the conversation with Julia. She noticed the change; she knew it would happen. It always did in the first stages. She didn't mind the slight distancing; the situation was just as unreal to her as it was to Stefan. They had only known each other for a grand total of twenty hours, yet, the fact they had developed that level of closeness was nothing short of a miracle. She also knew it was about the right time for fear to kick in, which generally led to abrupt severance. Someone would just get up and leave—no explanation. She had done it herself, but the guy across the table wasn't Stefan. Fear was for when things weren't right at the personal end. She was fine with him. Actually, she really wanted him to stick around. He was different, and in spite of his youth, she felt safe in his company. Also, he didn't seem to care that she was black, almost like he couldn't tell colors. That thought alone brought tears to her eyes. With José gone indefinitely, she had no idea how to proceed, but she trusted something would come up. People weren't destined to just die for no reason. Somehow, the power of the self, especially when the heart was clear and the mind focused, always emerged victorious out of struggle. She suddenly realized both had been following their own train of thoughts alongside the conversation. The reflection amused her; now she was ready to return to the focal point.

"You're feeling better?" she asked.

"Yeah, I lost my compass for a sec. I think I'll survive. I guess reality knocked at the door, but it turned out to be someone else's. Funny to say, but mine never left me; it was that I didn't own it. Now, I know it's here with me."

"Wow, that was quick, mister!"

"Quick thinking is part of emotional survival. Some get stunted by abuse, while others mature faster. I must be part of the lucky ones."

"I knew you were older than fifteen! But luck? I don't think it's luck; you can't randomize character."

"So, what do we do, Julia?"

"Alright, you hang out with me at Jimmy's—we'll stay out of his way. It's easy with his work schedule. We've got to provide our own food and contribute to some of the supplies, like soap etc... It's a start."

"I thought you two were an item...?"

"Hey, Jimmy's not crazy, I'm seventeen; he's like twenty-nine. Plus, I don't think he's into dating. I've never seen him with a partner, not even a dude."

"How long have you lived at his pad?"

"Just under a year."

"Don't you think it's possible he just needs emotional space while he figures things out?"

"I'm not saying he doesn't fuck, but he's never brought anyone to the place since I've been there."

A few of the usual suspects stopped by their table to shoot the breeze, and then moved on to where their stories could find better places to moor. One of them, by the nickname of *Small Butt*, squeezed one of Julia's breasts as if to check for firmness. She slapped his hand away, half annoyed and half amused. He laughed, congratulating her on its realness, and was gone.

"*Small Butt*'s just an asshole, if you don't mind the pun," she frowned.

"This place's full of characters. I've only been here a few times with my uncle, but I like it, creeps and all," Stefan remarked.

"Your uncle, is he cool?"

"Yeah, he's one of the good ones. So tell me, how did you end up being orphaned?"

"Oh my, I was afraid you'd ask... We lived in one of the North Marseille projects where most of the blacks and Arabs co-exist amid the effects of social decay and racial segregation. As you probably know, crime is fairly high down there. We were constantly awakened by the sound of sirens and firearms, sometimes machine guns. Anyway, one day my parents were having lunch at a small Italian eatery down by the flea market, when some dick threw a grenade in the joint. My folks were among the victims. Supposedly, it was an act of vendetta between Corsican families, but it could just as well have been some loony with a chip on his shoulder. I was four and my brother six. As the story goes, Social Services came to take us that same day, but somehow, they were unable to contact any members of the family in Dahomey, so we ended up in the care of the state. I never saw my brother again. Maybe one day we'll be reunited, but my hopes aren't very high. It's a tough world for a black kid, especially when crime is constantly knocking at the door. But who knows, maybe he landed in a rich family and is presently studying at Cambridge," she finished, a veil of sadness crossing her gaze.

It was exactly twenty-two hours. They got up and left for Jimmy's studio. It was agreed they would lift a few supplies at one of the all-night supermarkets on the way.

5 – PATROL CAR (Wed)

The brigadier at the desk of the central precinct watched Stefan's mug shot come out of the teleprinter. It was grainy, but sharp enough. It would join the rest of the dossier which had arrived from Fer earlier. He made copies of the print to post at the various substations, and then forwarded the original electronically to the two main newspapers. He rubberstamped "missing" in red across the top of the photos, and pinned one of them to the corkboard of the entry hall, below the flicker of a buzzing fluorescent fixture. One of the patrol cars would dispatch the rest of them at some later time.

It was a mere procedure. Most of the kids were either found within a couple of days or they returned home of their own volition after finding freedom was overrated—especially in winter. But as a rule, they mostly holed up with relatives. It was rare for runaways from nuclear families to completely vanish; when that happened, the cases were moved to the criminal branch.

Because of her mental history, Stefan's mother left a trail that automatically latched onto anything that touched her name. That explained why she emerged in the report as "psychologically unstable." Victor also appeared with the mention "violent," for reasons tied to previous complaints by acquaintances of those towards whom he showed a vicious tendency to not stop hitting when he should have.

"It looks like we may not get to this one too soon; his parents are all over the map. The lad could be invested in never seeing them again," the brigadier pointed to the other cop in the room, as he briefly glanced at the file.

"Nah, they're just dumb kids who don't know how good they have it. Look at this one's hair; I bet he drives his folks crazy!"

"You're just saying that because you can't get your wife pregnant. I bet you'd let your kids step all over you."

"You're probably right, I'm just mouthing off. But I haven't given up on Jane; maybe she's readying herself for twins or triplets?"

"Yah, you guys will get the timing right eventually. At any rate, make sure to keep an eye out for this kid when you go out," the brigadier finished.

The Renault 4L patrol car had barely pulled out of the lot when the dispatcher came on the air.

"Twelve, if you're just leaving, a suspicious teenager—male, long brown hair, medium height—was spotted going in and out of *Uniprice* without buying. The clerk claims the kid met with someone outside—about the same height—but it was too dark to identify the gender. Can you guys swing by?"

Chief Brigadier George Muller picked up the mic.

"I copy that; we're on it!"

By the time the car pulled in front of the supermarket, the suspects were gone. The clerk pointed in the direction he saw them leave, but he failed to convince the policemen that he had anything more than a case of assumption on his hands.

"Listen, we'll drive around the block a few times, and if we catch them with something of yours, we'll be back. Otherwise you have yourself a good night!"

George Muller was about to start the engine when he remembered Stefan's picture.

"Hold on a sec... you recognize this kid?" he asked, handing the print to the clerk.

"Kinda looks like him, but I could be wrong."

"At least you're wise enough to say you're not sure—thanks for your help!"

Muller, who was known for his sarcastic wit, wasn't particularly amused by seeing police resources misused by paranoid do-gooders. He felt the force was being taken for granted, same with firefighters. He calculated that nine out of ten calls were false alarms, which potentially took him off-course of real situations. So, as it turned out, the clerk observed a teenager patronizing the store that employed him; sure he didn't buy anything, but so what! Maybe he realized his mom didn't give him enough money for what she asked him to buy. Whatever it was, there was no wrongdoing. In his book, the only mischief came from the clerk. And now, it was all posturing and bending over backwards for a coward that had to be reassured that the fruit of his negligible tax contribution was being peeled and mashed for him in the name of personal gratification. He picked up the two-way radio microphone.

"Twelve over!"

"Go on George."

"Negative on the supermarket; we're on our way to the *Tower project*."

"Stay safe; they've been nervous lately up there!"

The dispatcher was referring to the *stups* sniffing for tracks of a large shipment out of Marseille on its way to Amsterdam. It also meant the town was flooded with

Moroccan hash, heroin, and with increasing presence, cocaine from Columbia.

Muller and his rookie keeper of the peace, David Witt, had no business crossing traffickers; that was the job of the *stups*. But jacked-up, small-time gang members were occasionally a dangerous nuisance, especially since they knew the cops carried bullets in a sealed pouch away from their unloaded *P38s*. But a few weary city cops had arranged to have access to seized ammo ahead of inventorizing. Consequently, and against regulation, some *Walther* sidearms were always ready for action. The way George Muller saw it, reprimand, or even demotion, was better than death. But then again, in all his time in the force, he never had to draw his gun.

6 – JIMMY'S PLACE (Wed)

Stefan and Julia had barely regrouped when one of the supermarket clerks was seen across the lot looking in their direction. The obvious reason Julia stayed out of sight was because she was too recognizable in a city with hardly any black residents. As a matter of fact, she shoplifted very little, and only during crowded hours. Part of Stefan's training was that he needed to build stealth through confidence, and just like everything else, it came with practice. Julia had briefed him on sussing the scene out in a manner that didn't arouse any suspicion. "Make it quick and use as much of your peripheral vision as you're capable of; you can't be seen shifting your gaze around nervously. If you're looking for something, make it seem like it's exactly what you're doing; you get the point. If you're compromised, don't do anything but leave. Now good luck!" she had said.

Stefan entered, quickly scanning the signs above the aisles. He ignored the personnel, but not without keeping a tab on them. He had just enough room in his winter coat for a couple of smaller items; anything more and it would give the appearance of extra bulge. When he located the cheese and packaged meats case, he did so while checking the large convex mirror high on the wall above it for floor activity. The coast was clear. He swiftly tucked a wedge of Appenzeller and a pack of smoked salmon against his chest, walked to the end of the display, hopped a couple of aisles over, and aimed straight for the exit, bypassing the line of registers. His heart was pounding, but he managed to maintain an air of nonchalance about his person, though it didn't quite convince one of the restocking clerks who rushed from across the store. When the worker reached the door, Stefan was already halfway across the lot, on his way to reconnect with Julia.

"I think you've been spotted, but the fact he didn't call after you means he's not sure whether you stole something or not. Did you?" she asked.

"Yep, I got a couple of things on the fly."

"Congrats! He probably deemed you suspicious because of your hair, but let's get outta here anyway; he might call the cops."

As they walked back in the direction of Old Town they saw the police car come their way. Luckily, they had just enough time to hide in the darkness of a recessed entryway before the vehicle passed them by.

"That fucker did call, I'm sure of it!" Julia uttered.

"So that's how it feels to live underground—a constant state of alert?"

"You got it, but you have it good; you could be black, and when you're black, that feeling is like a vise that tightens until you can no longer breathe."

"One of the few good things I learned from my dad is that blood is red regardless of skin color. During one of his best moods, he once said, 'If you ever married a black woman, or a Chinese woman, that would make me proud.' Too bad he's a fucking monster most of the time. But I'm sorry about how your people are being treated; it totally sucks."

"For some of us, it's gotten so bad that it doesn't matter what the white folks say; even the nice things become insulting."

"I hope you don't find it insulting if I tell you

31

you're great—I mean it!"

"Anything coming out of your mouth is music to my ears, so don't ever change your song, guitar man."

Before they came out of the shadow, Julia took Stefan's hand and squeezed it against her breast.

"I've been wanting to do that; now we can go," she said, smiling.

"I'll refrain from taking yours to my pants," he countered, laughing.

"Keep on refraining, naughty boy, there are better times and places for that to happen."

"Hey man, I checked the axe in your case while you were gone; not bad for an instrument made in Japan! We'll talk again—got to go to work!" Jimmy exclaimed as they crossed paths.

His steps reverberated inside the stairwell and the halls, followed by the creaking of springs and hinges, and then the soft mechanical clang of the catch, as the main gate was suctioned shut.

"It's nice to be home!" Julia exhaled, apparently relieved they had reached safe grounds.

Stefan put the fares away before the two huddled next to the radiator to chase the chill in their bones.

"Looks like the swelling of your lip is going down, but I'm sorry to say that the redness around your eye is turning purple. Lucky he didn't break your nose," she said.

"I'm prolly black and blue all over the place. He punched me in the guts and kicked me like a mad mule. When I was young; he broke his foot against the wall when I moved out of the way. There was enough force in the kick to kill me. I mean, I was only three or four—how can he live with it?!"

"The little I remember of my dad brings happy memories. I believe he was a compassionate man. Sometimes I think about how it would have been growing up as a family; I would have loved a younger sister."

"Sad to say there is very little that brings joy when I think about my folks. I love my sisters though, and I hope they make it through the madness."

"OK, I think I'm warm enough; time to cheer up! Fancy a cup? Jimmy's got some serious tastes in teas. I'm down for black; I can make a pot!"

"Please, I love tea!"

"While I get things ready, why don't you take a bath; I believe your body will thank you."

"Sounds lovely; anything I should know about the plumbing?"

"Elemental: hot is hot, cold is cold! Bubbles are under the sink; help yourself, they're mine!"

Stefan dropped his clothes into a pile on the white tiles of the floor. His penis was erect. He carefully entered the hot water until only the outer portion of his face emerged from the suds. He allowed himself to acknowledge that he was probably more exhausted than he was willing to admit—the thought amused him. The water felt great on his aches—he could have died right there and then, fully accomplished. But when Julia came into the room with a teapot, two cups, and a lit candle; shut the lights, took her clothes off, and joined him in the tub; only then did he realize what it meant to be truly accomplished. She faced him from across the bubbles, donning a mischievous smile of perfect teeth behind the most sensual of lips. He felt bedraggled from the beating and slightly ashamed by it, which, added to the soothing effect of the hot water, prevented him from spontaneously ejaculating from the pressures of the arousal. But when Julia guided his hand to her labia and clitoris as she reached for his hardened penis, his belly flexed in an uncontrollable spasm, his sperm shooting up through the foam, consequently leading to Julia's body being overtaken by a series of sustained orgasmic tremors. They both moaned from the unbearable pleasure, before joining in a long embrace. Finally, when their bodies settled into the calm of released passions, Julia leaned her back against Stefan's chest and reached to pour the still steaming tea into cups. As they sipped their brew, it had become clear that time could stop, or at least slow down to a very long wave.

That night, Julia and Stefan played with each other, merged with each other on undecipherable levels, and explored each other in places only they could reach, but at no time did they feel the urge to have intercourse. Julia confessed that she was afraid of it, because she had in fact been raped, not while on the loose, but by two of the older sons of the foster family she had been placed in when she was twelve—repeatedly raped. Stefan nearly cried from the news. He also shared that he never had been inside a woman. They slept in each other's arms until Jimmy had long returned from his shift and was buried in blankets.

7 – THE SPANIARD (Thu)

José Felipe Perez arrived from Seville in the summer of 1954 after crossing the Pyrenees along the Andorra border from Catalonia. He was a teacher and a member of the Internationalist Communist Party. As a passionate anti-Franco activist, he had been jailed numerous times for his involvement with the underground and was permanently marked by the dictatorship's crude methods of interrogation, notably in the form of deep-burn scars on his face and most of his body. He claimed that he never talked, and advocated death over disgrace. He married a French national and served in the Corps of Engineers in Trier, Germany, where he got into trouble for his work as a political organizer. Upon his discharge, he and his wife moved to Nancy, where they formed a network of safe houses for asylum seekers and runaways, which quickly spread over France, as well as into bordering northern European countries. Although, his intentions were noble, the money with which he financed the operation was less so. He ran the drug route between Marseille and Amsterdam, using Nancy as a hub that could additionally serve Paris to the west and Germany via Strasbourg to the east. It was rumored he dealt directly with the Columbian cartels responsible for the surge in cocaine availability across most of Western Europe. In spite of the scope of his dealings, he was approachable and ready to help anyone who needed a nudge in the right direction in life. His generosity of heart was epic, earning him the respect of those who were touched by it, including a very young Julia, who without *the others*, meaning those who worked under his guidance, might not have made it that far. The organization operated so stealthily, that even the authorities considered it a myth. The problem was the narcotics, which as it turned out, were substantially more visible due to the increase in publicity around the damage inflicted on its users and those around them; but even more importantly, by prohibitionists and various religious and business groups with political leverage, which saw in drugs, decreased attendance and diminished revenues, among other things. At least, that was how José and his wife put it, with the added bonus of believing those very groups were responsible for the steady increase in child pornography and traffic. To those who disagreed with his views, and they were many, the Spaniard was nothing more than a harmless fanatic; but in the eyes of the few who disliked him, he was a dangerous criminal. That few would have included the French Narcotics Brigade, or *stups*, if they had known who he was, but as close as they were to coming down on the organization, they had only identified lesser traffickers, those less likely to know José personally. In fact, what made him so invisible was the fact he didn't try to hide. His constant presence amid left-wing organizers made him a regular target of the news, and a repeat customer of the overnight tank following rowdy demonstrations. The cops knew him too well, which in an odd way, screened those he ushered to the safe houses from scrutiny.

Julia met José when she was transferred from a shelter in the South, following a routine raid of the project by Immigration. He had come down from Nancy in person to oversee the implementation of a bypass, which left the safe house permanently unoccupied, and thus, free of tracks. He took Julia with him and dropped her at a friend's place in the north-eastern city of Metz, wherefrom she hopped houses for the next two years, until she moved in with Jimmy. During that time, she saw José intermittently as he helped runaways, but she never was made aware of his involvement with drugs, at least not until she accidentally overheard a conversation with a contact from Holland. Metz was one of the lesser stopovers along the route, but it was a convenient place to meet for it being only an hour's drive from both Saarbrücken and Trier in Germany.

Julia quickly understood the Spaniard was trying to run more than just the safe houses, but she assumed the drugs were a new thing. So, when his place in Nancy was raided after she met Stefan, she took it that he had gotten greedy and acted against his better judgement, never connecting the dots to how he financed the runaways' network.

Though Julia was right in it being the *stups* and not Immigration that landed on José's abode, it was so on lesser charges of possession by one of his visitors from Spain. Actually, that day, he had been preparing for the demonstration on Stanislaus Square. The reason of his absence during the raid was because he had been antecedently arrested for riling the crowds, and spent the night in the tank. He was booked by no other than George Muller. Ironically, the *stups* had no idea how close they were. No drugs were found in the house and the visitor was released, pending some paperwork between France and Spain, which generally took forever.

José swung by *Le Thiers* upon leaving the station, as part of dispelling rumors and humbling the mystique about his person. In simpler terms, "shit happened," and the regulars were accustomed to leaving it at that.

8 – THE ARRANGEMENT (Thu)

At fourteen hours, Julia and Stefan met with José.

"I saw your face posted at the station; you know what that means, don't you?" the man told the teen.

"I'm not sure of the extent of it though," Stefan replied.

"It's simple, man: right know, there could be a plainclothes cop walking around this joint with a picture of your face imprinted in his brain, and within minutes, you'd be at the precinct telling your story, with 'sweet daddy' on his way to fetch you. You get the extent?"

"I get it I'm not safe in the open."

"Yeah, and that means just about any place in this town short of the morgue," José impressed on the youth.

"You're not just being sinister, are you?"

"I was told I had a penchant for the dramatic, but in a nutshell, for the next few days, you'll need to keep a low profile, which means no shoplifting. I'll speak with Jimmy, cuz you're gonna have to hole up in his place until the dust settles. Your picture will still be posted in the various stations, but soon the papers will stop publishing it, and the cops will easily forget about you. Your allowance is ten francs per day, there's enough here to feed you for a week. I will take care of Jimmy, while Julia will buy you some clothes; I'm sure you'll need to change your socks and underwear once in a while. So, you and Julia get outta here now; we'll meet in a week. As far as I know, you don't exist and neither do I, get it?"

After handing the money, he got up and left to join another table. The two walked out of *Le Thiers*. Julia suggested they stroll down to the zoo, where she believed Stefan would less likely be expected. As he saw it, he was in the hands of her educated guess—he trusted her.

Watching the lions mate wasn't exactly on the program, but it was interesting enough in that it lasted just about as long as the both of them playing in the bathtub; something like ten seconds. Nonetheless, the lioness rolled on her back with a growl, apparently overtaken with pleasure; but neither Stefan nor Julia thought the male enjoyed much of it. Maybe it was the sort of thing to do in the dead of a winter afternoon. Needless to say, it brought out giggles out of a group of young elementary school students, while the teacher went on venting her embarrassment by exclaiming, "You just saw what happened, right? Then be ready to talk about it in class!" which was immediately followed by more snickering; not the least of which was Julia's own.

As soon as the silliness subsided, the friends resumed with the pressing matters of existing under the radar. In Julia's case, since she was about to turn eighteen, there wasn't much the authorities could do to make her life miserable. On the other hand, Stefan had all to lose, knowing quite well that if he was sent back home, it would be a matter of time before the pattern of abuse found renewed footing, with redoubled strength and velocity. That probability ended against a wall of darkness.

"You understand there are things I do that will naturally exclude you," Julia abruptly said.

"Don't think I haven't thought about it."

"I'm not saying that's what's going to happen now, but I want to prepare you."

"I was prepared before you mentioned it, unless of course, you mean you're going away. Are you?"

"In time I will; but no, I just mean I have my ways and I'm used to them without another to cast their shadow over them."

"Not even when it comes with music?"

"That's not a shadow, silly, that's sunshine!" she laughed.

"Julia, d'you think of me as needy?"

"Not necessarily, but you're young, Stef, and youth has needs, especially the boys who seem to mature slower than girls. But again, I'm not saying it's you—you're kinda different that way."

"I always thought of my parents as emotionally arrested souls looking for father and mother figures in each other. It may sound odd, but I think my mother started searching for that parent quality in me—kinda sad and twisted, I'm sure. So, trust me on that, my youth's just a deceptive guise, if you know what I mean," Stefan returned.

"Are you saying I can lean on you?"

"You may try, but I kinda like my space too," he laughed.

"For the time being, we're stuck with each other. Normally, José would have taken you in, but with the latest fiasco, he's counting on Jimmy to cover for him. I'm sure that by now you understand how lucky you are that I came across you in the park. But as the saying goes, 'good things happen to good people.' Of course, I could say the same about me, Stef; I'm lucky you let me find you." Julia said, leading Stefan to the carousel.

"My English teacher once told us, 'There are no accidents, only the wish for them to happen.' I didn't know what he meant then, so I asked him to explain. He said, 'If you think about it hard and long enough, it will come to you!' I couldn't agree with him more today."

"But how can you wish for someone you don't know exists?"

"Not knowing they exist doesn't mean they don't. Our most silent wishes are those that hear the faintest of voices. Most of the time we're not aware those wishes exist either... All that to say there's much we don't know about."

"That's pretty deep, man. Is that the kind of stuff you think about when you lie in the dark?"

"Yes, among other things."

Jimmy was OK about the arrangement. Though it wasn't clear whether he was part of *the others* or not, or what exactly defined who these people were, Stefan assumed he was one of them. Maybe it was just a loose term to separate "the cool" from the rest.

"It's a good opportunity to practice your guitar, man—I'll teach you a thing or two based on where you're at. But there're a few things that need clarification: first, if you get caught, I don't know you, and neither do Julia nor José. It doesn't matter what you tell the cops, the tracks will be cold. If they ask you where you've been staying, tell them you slept in churches, or hung out at the train station; they won't care one way or the other as long as you don't involve people. The reason why we want to help you is because we've been there ourselves and we understand.

We know what awaits you back home—those kinds of bruises speak loud and clear, but they ain't the whole story; there's also the chance of psychological damage that eventually trickles down into society and keeps the cycle of evil going. It's a socio-political issue, but the law sees your protection from those patterns as a crime. It's utterly fucked, but there are places that get it, such as Sweden. Second, it's probably to your advantage that you get out of Nancy, cuz too many people know you in the area. Between your relatives and your friends and their parents, you'll get spotted in no time at all. Frankly, I'm kinda surprised it hasn't happened yet. So, you'll mostly have to stay in until we find you a safe place in another city, preferably a big one like Paris, Lyon, or Toulouse. Forget Marseille, they don't like long hair down there, plus being from Lorraine, they'll consider you German, and they fucking detest Germans. They still haven't gotten over the war, though there's irony in that... Anyway, history doesn't concern us for the moment. So, how d'you feel about what I just said, you're ready to take the plunge?" Jimmy asked.

"I am, but leaving Julia behind is kinda tough."

"You'll have plenty of time to explore each other before that happens, by then you'll realize friends are friends regardless of the distance between them. At any rate, I have matters to attend to, so I'll be gone for the night. The place is yours—feel free to help yourself with what's in the fridge—but please, no alcohol!"

Jimmy got up, grabbed his coat and keys, and left in a cascade of steps down the echoey stairwell.

9 – THE DEPOSITION (Fri)

The brigadier at the desk of the main precinct observed the elder woman walk up the hall towards him. She stopped by the bulletin board, looked up as if to verify something, and then proceeded in short steps accompanied by the scraping of her steel-enforced shoe soles against the tiles.

"Such a shame with all these *long hairs*; they probably never wash," she uttered, looking up at the officer from the vantage of her diminished form.

"How can I help you, Lady?"

"We sacrificed our lives fighting two wars, for what? My husband lost a leg for the county, you know; now look at what's happening to it!" she ranted.

"Unless you have a valid complaint, there's nothing I can do for you, ma'am," the cop stated.

"I've seen that boy in Old Town!"

"Which one?"

"The one from the paper, the girly one."

"Where in Old Town?"

"By St. Epvre's church."

"Please come into the office, so that Miss Schneider can take down your statement."

The woman dragged her feet towards the glass-paned door with the red-against-cream lettering that said, *Office*, opened it with feigned difficulty as to remind the clerk of his lack of courtesy, and entered to join a Miss Schneider who was in no mood to play the martyr ticket, having had to deal with pointless malcontentment on too many occasions to care about the woman's life story.

44

Nonetheless, the secretary assumed professional stance, offering a chair to the visitor, who oddly waited until the seat was pushed closer to her by one of the clerks leaving the room.

After painfully going over the section on name, address, and telephone number, the elder was asked to be more specific about her claim. She stated she had seen a *long hair* fitting the description by the record store behind the church. Miss Schneider reminded her that it was one of the places where the *long hairs* from town and the suburbs bought their records.

"The Devil's music!" she spat.

"So, what makes this one different from the others? You need to give me something so that we don't send someone there without a proper lead. You say he's the one in the photo, but for just a minute, forget about the print and describe him from your memory. In your estimate, how old was he?"

"I thought he was a girl, that's how old he was, sixteen at most."

"That's good! Now, how tall?"

"How would I know?! I don't go around measuring people!"

"Approximately."

"*A meter seventy.*"

"Low-medium then?"

"Well, they're growing so big these days; it's hard to tell for someone like me—they don't have a war to keep them short like my Julian."

"OK, then, what about his clothes?"

"Them blue jeans with the big bottoms, and a sheep's skin coat with the wool inside.

"Was he carrying anything with him, a bag, a

guitar case...?" the secretary pressed on.

"No, he just had his hands in his pockets."

"Was he alone?"

"There was a Negro girl nearby, but I don't reckon they were together. My Julian fought in the first war alongside Negro soldiers from Senegal; they used to cut the ears of the dead Germans fighters to bring to their families back home. He used to say that it stank the whole camp from across their unit!"

"Wonderful, but how does this serve this deposition?"

"I was saying, fighting a war together is one thing, but befriending these people is beyond common decency."

"Those are inappropriate comments that don't belong to this room. I'm sorry, ma'am, but you're going to have to keep your opinions to yourself. So, was this black girl with him or not?"

"A Negro girl and a white boy...?"

"That wouldn't be the first time, Lady. Are you sure your Julian fought for France?"

"Of course he did! What are you insinuating?"

"I'm only following the narrative, because it just so happens that my husband is a retired U.S. Air Force pilot—he's also black." Miss Schneider said sternly.

"To each their own, I said what I had to say!"

"Thank you for your time; we'll check the area. Good day! Patrick, please help this lady with her chair and show her the way out!" Miss Schneider requested of the clerk, rolling her eyes as she pulled the sheet from the typewriter.

"I think I've heard it all," she muttered to herself.

The elder woman was led down the hall, stopping

once again below the corkboard. She looked up and said, "My Julian would have shown you the whip; your parents should be ashamed of themselves!"

The scraping sound stopped with the closing of the main door.

"Brigadier Sterns, the kid may be hanging out in Old Town. Do we know a black girl in the area?"

"Even if she's in the files, we only classify people by name, not color. Without a name, there is little we can do. But the patrol team might know—if she's been around long enough, that is."

"It won't hurt to ask," Miss Schneider said.

10 – CITY OPTIONS (Fri)

Julia and Stefan woke up in each other's arms. The morning newspaper was open on the notices' page, where a picture of Stefan topped a small text. Jimmy wasn't buried under his customary pile of blankets at the opposite end of the room, rather, he had explained in a short note that he had gone for a ride in the country to visit his sister, and would be back by Sunday evening for his shift.

The lovers had spent a large portion of the night exploring the unknowns of their pleasure points, until they surrendered to exhaustion. Julia had requested once again that they hold off having intercourse, feeling she wasn't quite ready yet to trust a penis inside her. She was nonetheless fine with her partner's tongue socializing with the folds of her most intimate parts.

They got up and made breakfast. By the time the multiple cups of coffee kicked in, they were ready to open the page on the subject of social reality.

"I always wanted to live in Paris. I'm not sure how I would feel if I had to move to Lyon, Lille, or Toulouse," Stefan said.

"Unfortunately, it's not for you to decide. I mean, it's an issue of availability. I'm sure José's willing to hear you, but he's no magician."

"At this point, anything's better than life in Fer, that's for certain. I'm going to miss you though."

"Me too, Stef, I'm falling in love here..."

"What about moving together?"

"It's complicated—I promised myself to return to

Marseille as soon as I turned eighteen."

"What's in Marseille?"

"I want to find where my brother is. José was unable to locate him, which means that he either found a family or, if he ran off, he didn't meet with *the others*."

"Marseille's a big town, plus he could be anywhere, like England, as you said."

"I've got to start somewhere; Marseille's where it all began."

"But why didn't you look for him earlier?"

"Think for a second, Stef; what can an underage black girl on the loose do to get a search going? I have no legal grounds walking into a prefecture to seek answers, but everything will change in a couple of months. It's not like I didn't try; Marseille's where the tracks went cold."

"We'll have to visit each other then."

"Better I travel than you. You wouldn't last more than a day on the streets of Marseille before being picked up by the cops. They'll treat you like they treat my people down there; they hate hippies as much as they do the Arabs and the blacks."

"I guess it would suck to be a Moroccan hippie."

"Well, they do exist, musicians and other artists—same with Algerians and Tunisians—but they ain't kids and they have ways of defending themselves against the abuse of the system. They have their people inside, as well as lawyers."

"I never thought of myself as a hippie though, I'm more like a rocker," Stefan said, as if to try to correct a wrong.

"You go tell them! They're just assholes, high on power and fear," she returned.

"Fear?"

"Yeah, they get shot at regularly."

"OK, so you promise you'll come visit me then?"

"I will, Stef, I don't see how I wouldn't at this point. Of course, I'd love it if you could come with me to Marseille, but I don't want to see you hurt."

"Thanks, I understand... Meanwhile, we might as well take advantage of our time together, because I too am falling in love."

"I like the sound of it, Stef, but first thing first: José gave me money to buy you tees, briefs, and the likes. I hope it's OK by you if I pick the colors," she said, laughing.

"Be my guest, no-one but you will see them!" he laughed back.

An hour later, Julia exited the studio, leaving Stefan to practice his guitar. Earlier, he had played a few classical pieces for her; simple Ars Nova pieces learned by ear from records. She was enchanted. "It transports me to a world of magic..." she had cooed.

He ran through the same pieces again, pretending she was there by him, her eyes closed, while gently rocking her head side to side and rolling her hips on the cushion, as if she were dancing. He didn't want to say that he loved her, for fear of betraying the true meaning of love. He sensed love was much greater than two days worth of lustful attraction. But he loved her all the same.

Stefan began to worry when Julia didn't show up after being gone for three hours. He tried to convince himself that she probably had met with friends on the way to or back from the department store. He certainly didn't want to overreact; that surely wouldn't sit well with someone like her. But more time passed, and soon the last light of day fell behind the plateau overlooking the city.

"What are you doing here?!" José asked, not concealing his surprise.

"Julia never came back from her shopping run; she's been gone since one o'clock. She told me she would be away for an hour at most," Stefan explained.

"Fuck, you can't be seen in here with me—wait for me outside!"

Stefan stood in the cold, a small way away from the *Le Thiers* entrance, while José buttoned up what he had been involved with inside.

"Hey man, whattaya talking about; you're telling me she's gone?!"

"I wouldn't be here if I didn't think something was up; I've been waiting for her for hours," a distressed Stefan said.

"Calm down, bud, lemme think for a sec... OK, go back to the pad; I'll get in touch when I know something—got to call a few people!"

Stefan slowly walked back to Jimmy's place. An icy rain started to fall.

11 – JULIA'S ARREST (Fri)

Julia came out of the *Monoprice* store full of joy. She took delight in doing an errand for someone she cared very much about—something she had never done in her life. The sky had become overcast, but she took it in as another face of hope, one that didn't over-saturate its nature while blinding the mind. She was within visual distance of Jimmy's building when two men in cheap suits converged onto her from a side street.

"May we see your ID, Miss?" the shorter of the two asked, showing his badge.

"What have I done?" she questioned, knowing too well that running would only aggravate matters.

"We just want to see your ID card, nothing more."

"I don't have one; I lost it."

"You have a name?"

"Julia Feraez."

"Age?"

"Eighteen."

"Eighteen proper or seventeen going on eighteen?"

"The last one."

A patrol car pulled up to the curb.

"Sorry, but we have to take you in for identification. Don't even think of running off, there're four of us," the taller of the two undercover cops warned.

The patrol officer took Julia by the arm and propped her in the back seat of the Renault. His partner, David Witt, looked at her as if she were from Mars, but he was nice enough to ask her how she was doing and reassured her it was a mere formality.

"Just following orders, Miss," he said.

Julia was mortified. She didn't want to inculpate Jimmy and give Stefan away. She was going to have to lie, even though she abhorred lying. It was part of the code of ethics amongst those inside the réseau to do whatever it took to protect identities and the location of safe houses. She had prepared for such a moment, but with time, it felt as if it would never come. She held the bag of Stefan's clothes tight against her chest, a possession both precious and dangerous. How was she going to explain that she bought them for no-one in particular? She felt her blood leaving her face; her heart was pounding. "I'm so sorry, Stefan," she heard herself think, as tears ran down her cheeks.

The Renault pulled up into the station's courtyard. Keeper of the Peace, David Witt, led Julia by the arm into the interrogation room, where she would wait for the return of the plainclothesmen that had apprehended her.

"Are you sure you got the right one?" George Muller called from across the hall.

"Be nice, she hasn't done anything. Remind me one day, why we have to drag people like her in here without cause or warrants."

"I don't make the law, Sir, ask the brigadier!"

Julia waited for nearly an hour before she heard the steps and voices of the two undercover cops. In the meantime, Miss Schneider had been intermittently keeping her company, trying to make her feel at home by bringing her coffee and butter cookies.

"We're thankful you're managing to stay quiet. A lot of the youth we pick up can be rather belligerent. Some raise such hell that we can't even hear ourselves think," she laughed.

"I appreciate your attention, but I can't exactly say I'm thrilled by being here. I don't see much sunshine at the end of this tunnel. It's not easy to be me in a world that doesn't want me to exist," Julia said.

"Hey girl, you could be living in the U.S.; we're not so bad here. Take it from me, my husband is from Alabama and he's black. He's grateful to live a normal life in this country. So, cheer up!"

Julia relaxed somewhat. Miss Schneider was pretty cool for a cop.

The short one of the two was Major Ernest Jablonsky, while the tall one was Superintendent Jean-Marie Vidal, both hardened celibates, who, unbeknownst to them, were referred to as *The Couple*.

"OK, Miss Feraez, we're going to make this quick. We just need you to answer a few questions while we verify your identity, and you'll be on your way," Vidal said.

"Where do you live?" Jablonsky asked.

"Marseille."

"Marseille, hey? Are you staying with friends or relatives?"

"Neither."

"Neither meaning what, strangers?" Vidal probed.

"Yes, I met people yesterday, who are letting me crash on their couch for a couple of nights."

"We'll get to them later; do you know this face?"

Superintendent Vidal passed Stefan's photo to Julia, who looked at it with a bland stare.

"I don't recollect having met him."

"The reason you're here is because someone came in, who said you were seen with him."

"I understand there aren't many black people in this town, but I'm afraid it wasn't me. What has he done?"

"We normally ask the questions around here, but since you're from Marseille and you have no valid reason to know him, let's just say he's gone missing," Jablonsky said, acting the good cop.

"Since you don't recognize him, we're just going to wait for Miss Schneider to come up with your file and check your status. You understand that, at your age, you can't travel alone unless your parents or legal guardians give their approval. That's what we'll be looking into," Vidal explained.

The superintendent called Miss Schneider over the intercom.

"Olive, would you please call Marseille and see what we can unearth on Miss Feraez?"

In the meantime Major Jablonsky had been looking at Julia's shopping bag.

"What d'you have in there?"

"Underwear."

"Do you have a receipt?"

Julia handed him the receipt. The cop looked at it and gave it back to her.

"Looks legit, thanks," he simply said.

Julia felt the world below her cave in for a moment, but she was relieved by the fact she wasn't the subject of a search. It was just standard reflex on the part of the officer, who wanted to ascertain she hadn't stolen the goods.

"Superintendent Vidal, would you please come into my office; we may have a situation!" Miss Schneider was heard over the intercom.

Julia had been waiting for the moment at which the system would start telling truths about her life. That moment appeared to have come. She froze.

Jean-Marie Vidal left the room, while his partner kept a suspicious eye on the detainee. The energies had shifted, as if all that was round and soft in the room had morphed into sharp angles. The distant clickety-clack of typewriters was absorbed by a compressed and oppressive silence, which the drone of the fluorescent light ballast tried to penetrate. Time slowed to a crawl.

The superintendent returned to face Julia.

"Miss Feraez, unless you provide us with the name and address of someone who can be reached in this town and its larger area, and who can act as your custodian—either a relative or an adult friend of the family—I'm afraid we're going to have to book you until we can assess your status and connect with such a person. The Marseille police informed us that you vanished over three years ago after escaping from an orphanage. Can you confirm this for us?"

"Yes, I feared for my life."

12 – JOSÉ (Sat)

José Felipe Perez was rarely amused when the authorities interfered with the smooth process of his safe house operation. He loved Julia like a daughter, and there was no way he was going to let her be slapped around, so close to reaching emancipation age. It was clear to him that Stefan had something to do with it, but the kid wasn't to blame; he should have told the both of them to stay in and keep on fucking their brains out until the smoke dissipated. Now, he had no choice but fix the mess he was responsible for.

Saturday was never a good time to massage the system. Everything was closed, or whatever was open never answered the phone. Julia was most likely holed up at the main precinct, but it was Olive Schneider's day off, the one person he could talk to, also capable of keeping her nose out of his affairs.

But first, he had to swing by Jimmy's to reassure Stefan. He couldn't afford to have him walk the streets aimlessly, looking for her out of desperation. When he got to the studio, that what exactly what the kid was about to do.

"Chill, man, I'm on it! She's probably fine. Eighteen year olds don't get plucked out of the crowd in the middle of the day in a provincial city, maybe Marseille, but not here" José asserted.

"What happened to her?"

"I hate to lay it onto you, bud, but your face in the dailies didn't go unnoticed, and neither did your walks hand in hand with Julia. You tell me what's more visible than a white boy dating a black girl in an old, backwards German province? Sure, Nancy is pretty progressive, comparatively speaking, but it's the old folks you have to worry about; they've got nothing better to do than snoop into everyone's business, on top of still being grumpy about having had to live through two wars, while your kind is having fun changing the world." José pronounced.

A morose Stefan looked at the Spaniard as if he were from Mars.

"How are you going to get her out of jail; I mean, you just got out of it yourself?"

"Jail is a big word for an overnight cell. They're probably keeping her in there until they can find someone with the authority to get her out. It's my job to find that someone. But because it's the weekend, things are on standby, so she could be in there till Monday. At any rate, they have no legal grounds to keep her, she belongs to Child Services; someone from Marseille is gonna have to come up to take her back. We have to beat the system to prevent that from happening."

"And you can do that?"

"As you should know, the system is not a very integrated machine; some of the cogs are not meshing as they should, meaning, ghosts can travel through it, or, in simpler terms, there's a whole parallel reality of loopholes that exists within it."

"Gimme something cogent, José; this is too abstract for me right now."

"Please, don't go out unless you absolutely have to. Let me handle this, it's not my first time rescuing people. I'll keep you posted."

"OK, I'm crawling out of my skin though."

"Don't let commonsense crawl out of you, that's

all I'm asking. Just remember why you got me involved in the first place, so don't make me feel like I'm wasting my time—d'you get where I'm coming from, mate?"

"Fair enough, I'm done whining," Stefan said.

José was heard down the stairs speaking in Spanish with the concierge. Stefan suddenly realized that the man' appearance concealed something extraordinary as well as potentially dangerous.

Olive Schneider had a hard time sleeping that night. She kept on going over the case of the black teenager. How could the girl have skipped the radar for so long? The files had arrived via telex towards the end of her shift, and since no-one would be dealing with them over the weekend, she took them home. She had no business doing so, but Chief Brigadier Muller and *The Couple* would not require them, and those were the only ones she needed worry about. The girl was to remain at the station anyway, at least until *Social* would step in.

What she learned was that her parents had been murdered and that she had been separated from her brother, whose tracks vanished long ago. Other details, only someone in the investigative world would have noticed, showed inconsistencies: the chronology of her time between the orphanage and the families she was placed in was missing data, as if someone had gone in there and removed it. There was a whole one-year period that was absent from the list. She also noticed there was no report of her time prior to her escape from the orphanage; no psychological evaluation that could have shed light into the reasons behind it. It didn't look like protocol. She couldn't afford to be accusatory, for it ran counter to professional standards, but it looked like some tracks had been erased with the single purpose of protecting specific identities. Schneider found the act remarkable in the light of such tinkering yielding exactly the opposite result; instead, it drew her to suspect near-incontrovertible wrongdoing.

It wasn't names that she was interested in, but the reasons why the dossier had been tampered with. Julia ran from something, and it certainly wasn't the promise of a better future. "I feared for my life," she had said. The words still rang like cold steel in the secretary's mind.

Olive Schneider wasn't just a secretary working at the police station; she was actually an officer of the force, and a superior of George Muller. She didn't have the leverage of *The Couple*, but she could raise dust when dust needed raising. Not that it necessarily meant much considering she was still a woman in a man's world, but her strong personality and unquestionable wits made for sustained respect among those very men.

Her husband, Bernie, was at a reunion of World War II U.S. veterans and she had the whole week to herself. When the phone rang, she assumed it was him calling, but she quickly recognized the accent and wondered why José Perez would be ringing her on her day off.

"Sir, I assume you wouldn't be calling if you didn't need something," she cut, before he had a chance to state the reasons of his untimely interference.

"It's kind of an odd story. Someone has been

looking for a black teenager from Marseille, claiming she went missing. I told him to use the proper channels, but he insisted he didn't want to involve you guys."

"Odd to say the least, since it doesn't make much sense he would be asking you to help him. I gather that someone has a past to protect; but why you, may I ask?"

"I know a lot of people, that's why."

"You know, you've been around long enough to have earned a modicum of respect from me, and by that I certainly don't mean through your wild megaphone shenanigans on the main square. I'm aware of what you went through with that bastard Franco, and, as I see things, you have the kind of education that puts a lot of value into a man. So, that's why I have come to feel a certain fundamental sympathy towards your person, which of course, doesn't mean you can call me in the privacy of my home with a bogus story any time you wish. So, what's the deal here, José?"

"OK, Miss Schneider, as you wish. I know the girl, I also know she went to Hell and back—she could use a break. It's all I'm willing to say in that regard. Now, 'a man from Marseille' may visit the station, claiming he is a relation of hers. That's where you come in. The relative in question will be an impeccably dressed black gentleman with excellent manners, but he won't be able to provide the kind of credentials that would normally be requested of him for the release of the detainee into his custody."

"You have a lot of nerves; what you're asking of me is beyond indecent. I could press serious charges against your person for it. You're technically trying to corrupt an agent of the force; are you not aware of it?!"

"Hence the seriousness of the matter. As far as I

know, this call never happened and you have no means to prove it did. You're well aware that involving the authorities into this is bound to backfire. I hate to remind you you're a woman working for the man, and don't tell me that in your heart, you consider it to be a leveled field. They will only pretend to take you seriously, and you'll be wasting your energy in spite of your superiority. I'm only asking you to be fair, not to go against your own judgement. Let's just say, you forgot something at the office. The gentleman will be there tomorrow at three."

"You have it all planned out, haven't you? You're right, this call never happened. Bye!"

13 – THE CELL (Sun)

Julia was awakened by the sound of patrol cars leaving the courtyard outside her cell window. The flip clock in the guard's office said 05:34. She hadn't slept well, not just because of the hard cot or the single blanket that couldn't keep the chill away, but because her mind had been racing all night. Again, she wasn't particularly worried about herself, but the idea of compromising Stefan, José, and Jimmy, as well as countless others down the line, tormented her. She tried to reason the self with the reminder that she wasn't the first runaway to get nabbed, but somehow she couldn't shake the wave of nervous energy that was aiming at deconstructing the physics of her being.

In the early evening, a line cook from the Charles III prison had come to deliver her dinner of mashed potatoes, meatloaf, green salad, brie, and apple pie. She had felt comforted by the food even though she, at first, hadn't wanted to touch it.

She had missed the four o'clock guard relief. The new guy was a rookie barely out of his teens, with round, red cheeks and slightly puckered lips. He was reading a sports car magazine, showing no interest in her.

Her breakfast arrived at half-past six sharp—she was actually hungry.

At seven, there was some commotion coming out of an office down the hall. There were yells. A man was being brought in on charges of public drunkenness. Julia heard the slammer of a cell door; the insults subsided.

It was raining hard against the yard's cobblestones,

63

as water came gushing out of greened copper drainpipes. It was that kind of morning, a picture of grey awakening from darkness; a rain-drenched picture of urban melancholia that resonated with Julia's inner emotional landscape.

Another man's voice was heard addressing the desk clerk. Soon afterward, Superintendent Vidal entered the cell.

"I want to make sure you are being treated well before I leave town. I shall be back tomorrow; by then I'm sure we'll be in position to resolve your situation. Marseille is sending someone to take care of the paperwork, and hopefully you'll be on your way."

"Whom from Marseille?"

"Most likely someone from Child Services; I spoke with Superintendent Schmitt who used to have my job here—you're going be in good hands."

Vidal got up and left.

It was the last thing Julia needed to hear, "to be in good hands." It sounded like a twisted code name for "death sentence." She had planned on returning to Marseille down the line, but not sandwiched between cops, or possibly worse, thugs passing for Social Service employees. She started to contemplate how she was going to have to lose them before they reached destination. She didn't care how short her ordeal would be, there was no way she would leave Stefan under such humiliating conditions. In the meantime, she hoped for a miracle.

Lunch came at the ring of the cathedral's bells. She thought of the congregants, as well as those who went to mass with the single goal of hitting the bars after the service, to indulge in the ritual of the sacred aperitif. She remembered how fond Stefan was of the term *absurd*—she saw herself caught in a marriage of *abstract* and *absurd* aimed at depriving them of the love they had for each other. The thought left her the same way it had entered her mind. She poked at the aspic.

To Julia's surprise, Miss Schneider entered the cell at half-past fourteen. The secretary wasn't due till eight, the next morning.

"A superior from Marseille called on the home emergency line to let me know someone was coming for you this afternoon. No rest for the wicked!" she uttered.

"Already? The superintendent told me it wouldn't be until tomorrow."

"What do we know? Believe me; I hadn't planned on coming to work on my day off!"

"So, they're taking me back to Marseille?"

"That's where you said you lived, didn't you?"

"Yes."

"You're sure about it, I hope, because it wouldn't be to your advantage to end up in the wrong town?"

Julia kept silent.

"What did you mean by 'I feared for my life'?"

"They told me they'd kill me if I talked."

"And you were fourteen at the time, right?"

"Yes, and younger when it first happened."

"So what went down then?"

"I was raped by the men they sent me to."

"Who sent you?"

65

"The orphanage, the nuns."

"What about later?"

"I was molested and beaten for resisting until I passed out."

"By whom?"

"One of the main nuns."

"Have you ever told anyone about it?"

"I've told a friend."

Olive Schneider reached to hold Julia's hand.

"I understand you will be turning eighteen soon. Would you be willing to give a deposition if I asked you to then? I think it's important that these actions come to light—of course, you'd be put under police protection."

"I might consider it, but I'll be in Marseille then."

"Perhaps you don't have to be in Marseille."

"What do you mean?"

"I'm just saying... I think it's time I get to my office to prepare for our visitor."

Jean-Michel Tourbé entered the station at exactly the time he was expected. He was tall and stately, bordering on intimidating. He went straight to the clerk at the desk, introducing himself in a guttural voice. He was asked to take a seat in the waiting room. Miss Schneider soon came out, shook his hand, and asked him to follow her in.

"So, Mister Tourbé, what can I do for you?"

"I'm Julia Feraez's uncle; I believe I came to the right place."

"Indeed, may I see some identification, please?"

Tourbé handed over his ID. Olive Schneider

pretended to scrutinize it, absentmindedly looking at the man's photo. She returned the card.

"What proof do you have of your relation with Miss Feraez, since Child Protection Services didn't inform me of your visit?"

"Miss Julia has been under my care since she left the orphanage. I took her in after she was badly battered. She has been traveling across France to look for her brother Amadi."

"What makes me believe you aren't one of the people who might seek to harm her?"

"It's simple; I'm not part of the institutionalized system of corruption that wants her back. Tomorrow, a man and a woman from 'Services' will officially take her into their custody and you will never hear of Miss Feraez ever again. But I trust you wouldn't be here today if you didn't want to act in her best interests," the man said.

"You will have to fill up a couple of forms ahead of me releasing Julia in your care. But before we get started, I'm going to call her into the room. If I sense anything indicating she doesn't recognize you or doesn't want to go with you, the deal is off."

"Fair enough," the man agreed.

"Weber, could you please bring Miss Feraez over into my office!" Olive Schneider instructed the guard over the intercom.

Julia entered the room. She immediately recognized the man sitting in the chair. He was one of José's safe house liaisons from Metz, with whom she had interacted on a number of occasions. She smiled at him, but chose not to say anything for fear of compromising him. She stood, waiting.

"Your uncle, Jean-Michel, was nice enough to

come for you on such a rainy day!" the secretary uttered, inconspicuously providing information she knew Julia didn't possess.

Tourbé filled in the paperwork, while Julia gathered her things and freshened up in the bathroom.

After wishing them good luck, Olive Schneider watched them walk down the hall, until the main door closed behind them.

"God help me!" she thought aloud.

14 – RESCUE (Sun)

Julia and Jean-Michel Tourbé got into the Citroën GS and drove off.

"It's nice to see you, Johnny. I don't know how you and José pulled this one off, but it's rather impressive!"

"It wouldn't have happened without Miss Schneider's help; I hope she doesn't get in trouble."

"She looked like she was just doing her job."

"Not really, she had no business being there on a Sunday. She also knew Protective Services were on their way; she's gonna have a lot of explaining to do."

"I guess I owe her one."

"You owe a lot of people, girl!" he laughed.

"She told me she wanted me to come back after I turned eighteen to talk about what had happened down in Marseille."

"Yes, she knows something's up."

Julia realized they were driving out of town.

"What's happening, Johnny, why are we going this way?"

"Jimmy's compromised. Miss Schneider had no choice but to have us followed as part of erasing some of her tracks. Taking you back to your pad would have led the wolf straight to the sheepcote. Our best option is to drive out of town; we're going to Toul."

"What's in Toul, and what's going on with Stefan? Julia asked, panicked.

"I live there now and I'm in good standing with the community. I teach at the high school, so the visit of a family member isn't going to raise suspicion. As far as Stefan's concerned, José's on it—they should be at the house by the time we arrive."

The twenty kilometer ride was slowed by icy rain. The ghost of the old gothic cathedral stood massive above the town's rooftops. Toul was the last place Julia would have thought of going, a city of fifteen thousand on a bend of the Mosel River, and according to her, a dead community gone deader since the closure of the U.S. Air Force base.

"It's not that bad; we have a couple of rock bars, some pretty good local bands, and plenty of history to unearth if you're into that kind of stuff. Here we are!" Johnny said, as he pulled up in the front yard of an old stone farmhouse on the edge of town, next to José's car.

Johnny's wife, Suzanne, opened the door to let them in.

"Welcome! José, Stefan, and the kids are in the living room; please take your shoes off. I assume you two would like something warm to drink, I have a pot of fresh coffee brewing."

"Thanks, love, I'm sure Julia could use a cup!"

The energy between Julia and Stefan approached the igniting point. Suzanne was particularly receptive to it during a flash of focused awareness. José approved with a conspiratorial wink and a broad smile made all the more genuine by the scars on his face. The Spaniard, who valued passions above all things, was deeply touched by the gift returned for his efforts, one of love between two unique individuals rescued from the hands of an ominous fate—he felt like a savior. Suzanne and Johnny's twin boys were all over him, squealing from a mix of pleasure and excitement, while trying to escape the imaginary monster that was chasing them across the room on all fours. Uncle José, as they called him, was a high point in their lives, and he absolutely adored them.

Suzanne returned with the coffee to join the group around the serving mat; she sat across the teenagers.

"I have prepared the converted barn for you two, I hope you don't mind sharing the same space; it's only one room with a small attached bathroom, but it's warm and cozy. The only problem is in crossing the courtyard in the rain; it's also slippery," she said in a soothing voice.

Julia and Stefan unloaded their belongings out of José's car and carried them to the old converted barn. The Spaniard wanted to go over a few things before returning to Nancy. The three of them sat in the loft overlooking the small living area where a potbelly wood stove hissed, growled, and crackled with life.

"You two will be staying here for a while. I haven't had the time or the energy to survey what's available out there, Stefan; and now that Julia needs a place too, it might take a bit longer. Julia may still be able to go out, but mate, I'm sorry to say that you'll have to bear with it, cuz as far as the fuzz's concerned this is merely the city's outer suburbs. I mean, you could practically walk to Fer from here; though I wouldn't do it!

At any rate, I was thinking Strasbourg might be a good fit, and it's not too far. I'll keep you posted as soon as I come across something."

"What happened at your house, José?" Julia asked in a low voice.

"It was nothing; just one of my careless stoner friends visiting from Spain, and getting busted with a couple of grams of hash. I don't even know why the cops even bother."

"Be careful, José, lots of kids need you. I don't want you to get in trouble with the law."

"Thank you, sweetie, but José knows what he's doing, even if it appears like he doesn't. Nonetheless, I promise to not do something I might come to regret; please trust me."

"A promise's a promise, right?" Julia insisted.

"Count on it, baby girl, I wouldn't lie to you; but let's move on! Alright, it's understood Johnny, Suzanne, and the twins are busy trying to be a family, so I depend on you to show them due respect. They're good people, warm and generous, and above all, they're willing to help you until I get you out of here. So, give them a hand with things, like, wash the dishes, clean the chicken coop; I mean, offer your services—that will go a long way! OK, I'm outta here—Hasta luego!"

15 – VIDAL'S IRE (Sun-Mon)

Olive Schneider went over Julia's release paperwork; everything appeared in order. Vidal would be furious about it, but there was nothing he could do, knowing the proper channels had been used. Of course, there was going to be an incidence of confusion with Child Services, but then again, the system had been known to be afflicted with much more absurd situations. It was mostly that the superintendent detested interference in his affairs; thus, he was going to inquire on the reasons why she had not tried to reach him on his buzz pager. She would come up with something.

But there were more pressing things on her mind, namely, the corrupted dossier from Marseille, and what Julia had confided in her. It wasn't her first instance of coming across perplexing omissions in regards to related matters. For the last two years, she had been conducting a private investigation, gathering as much data as she could. She suspected a ring, or multiple connected rings to be responsible for the disappearance of orphaned children and runaways, through their dealings in pornography, prostitution, and enslavement. As she went deeper into the layers, it became obvious the level of corruption was such that some public figures had to be shielded; meaning their minions had infiltrated the system, including the force. She was aware of possessing information not necessarily safe in the hands of her superiors. José was right by saying they would only pretend to take her seriously. Most likely, the importance of her work would be minimized, or if not, time-tested rationale such as,

"We don't have enough for a case," would be tossed her way. She had heard it all before, thus something of imposing mass had to be built before the official channels could be exploited.

There was also the mystery of José. How did he know she would let Julia go? And who was Jean-Michel Tourbé? Certainly, it wasn't his real name. The fact he and the Spaniard had known the girl for some time, indicated they had been protecting her from the same people she was trying uncover. *How* and *why* were at the nexus of the enigma surrounding the two men. They took a great risk by exposing themselves to her, gambling on the odds she would be seeking to protect Julia as well. There was something larger than life looming in the background. And what was the deal with the teen from Fer? Was José also protecting him? Stefan Vogt was no orphan, just a rebellious kid from a blue collar town, like countless others with abusive folks and an attraction to early freedom. But his mother had been parentless, and based on her profile, the way she came out of it showed the nuns and her foster parents weren't kind to her—a small link, but one nonetheless.

Olive Schneider came to the conclusion she needed to know more about José Felipe Perez. His past was no secret, but the present hid too many shadows. Tracing the source of his income was a priority. He appeared to have a lot more free time than most, based on his involvement with leftist politics. It was certain he wasn't getting money from the party; they could barely pay for the paper on which they printed their news and fliers. Maybe his wife made enough money as a teacher for the both of them, and perhaps, he was still teaching on the side. Still, without evidence, it was all speculation.

She filed Julia's dossier and left the station. No use to pretend there was more work to do; tomorrow would come soon enough and it wouldn't matter then.

Superintendent Jean-Marie Vidal arrived at the precinct, at nine forty-five, accompanied by the two CPS agents he had picked up at the train station.

Schneider promptly informed them that Julia Feraez had been released in the custody of her uncle the day before.

"Her uncles are in Dahomey and none of them have shown any interest in caring for her. They've never even responded to our requests," the woman by the name of Monique Colbert said coldly.

Vidal was livid.

"Who authorized?!" he spat.

"I did. It just happened I was here fetching the gift I had bought for Bernie that I forgot on Friday,"

"And?!"

"This big black man showed up, saying he was her uncle, and that he had learned she was being detained here. I asked for his ID, questioned him for accuracy, and introduced Julia to him, which confirmed the two were related. Since Miss Feraez was only held for the time it would take us to verify her status, nothing in protocol prevented me from releasing her. It was just a happy coincidence that I was here when he came in."

"Don't throw protocol at me, Schneider; you knew

damn well these people were coming today! And what about calling me?"

"I tried, but your service must have been down because of the storm."

"OK, so some power poles came down because of the ice; wasn't there anyone here who could have taken care of business when you were supposed to be home?"

"Sorry, but I was the highest ranking officer at the time; it was my job to make the decision. The release documents are in the cabinet; you may wish to go over them for evidence of wrongdoing," Schneider said firmly.

"We're going to need a copy of those papers, Miss. If Superintendent Vidal doesn't find anything wrong with them, we might," the CPS man said starkly.

"I take it that returning Miss Feraez to Marseille is of particular significance to your superiors, but I stand by my decision. I trust she is presently in safe hands."

"I shall make due notice of it in the report," the man returned.

Vidal looked at the secretary menacingly.

"We'll need to talk after I return from bringing agents Visconti and Colbert back to the station!"

The return came promptly, accompanied by the obligatory dust-raising common to bruised egos.

"Bravo, Schneider, you've managed to make us look like a Mickey Mouse operation. Now, I've got to clean up your mess, so that we can show we have a modicum of integrity!" Vidal lashed as he entered.

"With all due respect, Sir, we're the National Police; since when do we answer to Marseille?"

"You know what, Schneider, you're making this personal. Oh, I understand, black husband, black girl; but beyond sentimentality, we have an obstruction case!"

"How can you say that; she wasn't under arrest, and she's only two months away from turning eighteen? What's wrong with her uncle showing up and taking her home?"

"Her age is of no consequence to Marseille; they would be glad to let her loose if they didn't think she could help them. She might have information they need in solving a highly sensitive case, and you've just messed that up. We're called the National Police, because we operate on a national level. Now, I've got to explain, not only to Marseille, but Paris headquarters as well, why Nancy has gone rogue!"

"I see, I suppose I should bear the blame for you keeping that information to yourself."

"I have my reasons and they're purely professional."

"Then I have to take it that you deem this unit untrustworthy of assisting in a critical investigation."

"Perhaps, Schneider; but for the time being, consider yourself lucky that I shan't seek to have you transferred. Meanwhile, we've got to find Feraez."

The office door slammed shut behind him.

Olive Schneider got up, opting for an early lunch. The rain had relented, so the prospect of a walk to the eatery was welcome. The fresh air would clear her mind. Halfway to the restaurant, she decided on a hunch to go to *Le Thiers* instead. She sat at the counter, ordered a ham sandwich with a *grand crème,* and surveyed the room. Her lunch arrived just as José Perez entered the busy space. He sat next to her.

"It might appear reckless on my part to be seen in your company, but I want to thank you for what you did yesterday," he said.

"It's my job to make sure the innocent are feeling safe under my watch. It is also my duty, as a human being, to weigh in the merits of the law when that safety is jeopardized. When I saw Julia smile at Jean-Michel, I knew she would be alright with him; I didn't necessarily hold the same feelings for what was awaiting her the next day. I'm sure I did the right thing. But now, you and I have to talk, not at the station, but away from scrutiny. I have a feeling my phone is no longer private, while yours, as you probably know, is monitored at all times. What do you say we meet out of town for lunch tomorrow? I will make reservations at the *Restaurant des Vannes* in Liverdun."

"If it's your thing to drag a rabid leftist into a bourgeois institution, you chose well—why there?"

"It's the last place one would expect to find us."

16 – MORNING IN TOUL (Mon)

Julia and Stefan got up early. They joined Johnny, Suzanne, and the twins in the lively bustle of the kitchen for breakfast.

"We know much about Julia, but what's your story, Stefan, if you don't mind me asking?" Suzanne probed.

The teen described the best he could the chain of events that had led to Julia finding him asleep on a park bench.

"So, you believe that if you were to return to your family, the abuse would potentially worsen, am I right?" Johnny cut in.

"'Worsen' is kind of a surreal concept, because it has already worsened to the point of unbearable. If I didn't think my dad could inflict irreversible damage, I probably wouldn't be here now."

"How long has that been going on?"

"Until recently, I thought it began when I was around ten, but now I'm starting to recollect memories of earlier abuse, not just physical, but verbal as well."

"If you don't mind me moving on—we can always get back to it later—you're obviously quite intelligent and focused; how have you been faring with your studies?" Johnny asked.

"Back in the day, I was always top of my class, but now I don't care anymore. It's funny, or maybe it's not, but my mother had set me up with a piggy bank. If I came in first on the monthly test, she'd give me five francs; second, I'd get four; and down to one franc if I came in fifth. For years, I received five francs every month. Then, when I asked for the money, because I had a purchase in mind, I found out that my dad had helped himself with it—there was nothing left."

"Did you ask for it back?" Suzanne asked.

"I tried, but he wasn't impressed. All he said was, 'Are you gonna sue me?!'"

"I see."

"I mean, I was twelve; what was I gonna do? He looked like he was ready to hit me if I spoke another word. After that, school didn't mean anything to me anymore. I only loosely studied for the tests."

"You heard it, Suzanne, another home-spun tragedy!" Johnny exclaimed in disgust.

Johnny dropped the twins at the kindergarten on the way to his high school teaching job. Suzanne was studying for her nursing degree, so she set up at the kitchen table, capitalizing on the brightness and comfort of the warmest room in the house. Julia and Stefan were washing and drying the dishes that had accumulated since the night before. The hostess' love for helpful company was returned in heartfelt kindness. She was supportive as well as engaging, emanating a contagious wellness of being. She touched and hugged as in saying, "You're family—you're welcome here as long as you wish."

When Johnny and the twins returned for lunch, the table had been set, with food ready to be served.

"It's lovely to have help!" Suzanne rejoiced.

The boys ran around the table, laughing and screaming, until they were reminded what the kitchen was for. Eventually, everyone found their place. The ambiance of the meal was sparsely accented with the latest on world and local news, mostly politics. When Julia asked if he had heard about the weather forecast, Johnny's response was, "It's just for fools and flatlanders; we've got windows for that. For now, it looks like cold rain, but you're welcome to disagree." Of course, he was playing, but Julia got the point he wasn't too fond of the weatherman.

"I would love to take a walk into town; that's why I asked," she said.

"We may have better luck tomorrow," Suzanne offered.

"It doesn't matter to me; I'm on a guitar practice regimen," Stefan humored.

"Stefan, the one thing we haven't spoken about yet is that we deem education to be a vital tool in the fight against social biases. We try to highlight its importance to the teens that go through us. When you guys turn eighteen, we don't want you to land out there unequipped; that would defeat the purpose of what José, myself, and many others have strived to accomplish. So, alongside your guitar practice, which by the way is part of a noble branch of education, I would suggest that you keep up to date with your present studies, namely languages, since I hear you're taking German and English," Johnny stressed.

"Don't forget math, world history, geography, and politics!" Suzanne contributed.

"I guess biology isn't on the list," Stefan remarked playfully.

"No, you're not going to be dissecting live things or study cadavers, if that's what you mean, but I advise you take physics instead," Johnny replied tit-for-tat.

"What about you, Julia, how are you doing with your schooling?" Suzanne inquired.

"I think I'm up to date with most of it. Lucky I was able to practice my English with a couple of runaways from Brixton, but I heard it might work against me in the long run, since no-one understands them outside London," she laughed.

"The French can't tell the difference, anyway," Johnny said.

"You mean because they don't speak English, or because they don't have an ear for nuances?" Stefan asked.

"To call heavy Cockney a nuance might be a stretch, Stefan, but all the same. An Irish friend of mine from Cork once wondered how I could possibly understand him when the English couldn't. It's not because the ear can hear that the mind listens. Belief and prejudice are stumbling blocks to communication. The French have their own issues with those they choose to ignore."

"But we can change the world by welcoming love in our hearts and homes," Suzanne said.

"Amen to that!" Johnny seconded.

17 – THE MEETING (Tue)

Olive Schneider waited for José on *Place de l'église* in Liverdun. She knew the area well for having been raised in the small commune. It was also where she met her husband Bernie, who at the time was stationed at the Toul-Air U.S. airbase barely a mile out of town, up on the plateau overlooking the Mosel River.

José parked his Citroën 2CV by the presbytery. They walked the short distance to the restaurant.

"I forget how quaint this place is, even on a grey day," José voiced, aiming to cut the ice.

"I grew up here. I attended kindergarten down from the vicarage. It was run by nuns back then. One of them, Sister Marie, was a sweetheart; she was very old and kind. The others were mostly harpies. I was hit once by a wiry one from Belgium, for commenting on her spitting in the holy water when she talked, while she was actually lecturing on the blasphemous practice of spitting in the font. No wonder most of us have gone atheist."

"Same in Spain, the church is its own worst enemy. Their *do as we say* pontificating is no longer keeping the masses blind to the *not as we do* side of things. Times are a changing!"

"You may say that, Sir, but here we are; I believe our seats are calling us!"

They were shown into a nearly full room. Somehow, the bad weather had not deterred the patrons.

"The bourgeoisie exists in a parallel universe within ours," José whispered.

"Mind your manners, mister; now is neither the

time nor the place for politics!"

The bourgeoisie in question were no other than the wealthy owners and directors of the factories and processing plants that lined both sides of the river. The restaurant was the place where obscure deals and alliances running counter to the general discontentment that saw the resignation of President Charles de Gaulle the year before, were made.

"I'm glad you're wearing a decent outfit like I asked," Schneider remarked, as they were being seated.

"I have slept with the enemy before."

"I'm treating, so don't be shy. I've also taken the afternoon off—I hope you're in no rush."

"Does it mean something dark is looming?"

"There are a number of things on my mind that concern both you and our so-called protégés; the direst of them being that Superintendent Vidal has issued a search warrant for Julia and Jean-Michel Tourbé."

Olive Schneider anticipated a facial response, but José didn't flinch.

"It sounds like your superintendent has a few skeletons in his closet."

"Or that he's got something to prove—he might simply have a small town complex."

"Is that an office pun?" José asked sarcastically.

"We'll bring the skeletons out when we get proofs; for now let's put a few cards on the table. I may respect you, Mr. Perez, but that doesn't mean I trust you. So, before we start getting cozy with each other, you may want to elucidate on the one mystery that plagues your person: how do you make your money?"

"I like candid, but trust goes both ways in a healthy relationship."

"I chose this place to make sure you knew this wasn't an interrogation; and just in case you didn't pay attention, I'm not exactly following protocol," Schneider replied coldly.

"Fair enough, I receive money in exchange for my work in an underground operation, to mostly finance a brainchild of mine."

"By underground, I'm inclined to believe that you mean criminal, am I right?"

"That would depend on what side you serve. As far as I have observed, some of criminality is defined by laws created by criminal for criminals. My kind of underground leans more towards restoring balance."

"It's just semantics, José... May I call you by your first name if I let you call me Olive? What I'm saying is that it doesn't matter whether you're right or wrong, the law is blind to individual interpretations of justice."

"But between you and I, and in this place, we don't have to pretend that we are governed by immutable rules. Perhaps, as part of the trust you ask for, we could start by cutting down on the bullshit. What is it that you want, Olive?"

"You're right; I need your help."

"And so could I use yours."

"It sounds like a good time to raise a toast; here's to trust!" Olive Schneider cheered.

While his companion was busy in the powder room, José analyzed the logistics of Vidal's warrant for Julia and Johnny's apprehension. There was no Jean-Michel Tourbé; Schneider had just gone with the motions, for she most likely had already assumed his ID card was forged. So, technically, Johnny could not be traced. The problem was with Julia, who was free to move around town. Toul was way too close for comfort, and it was likely Vidal had already informed the local gendarmerie. Since the town was a straight shot from Liverdun, he would drive there after the meeting. As far as he was concerned, phones came with too many eavesdroppers to be trusted. Johnny was black; it didn't take a genius to figure out his line was tapped; and even if it wasn't, why would he chance a call?

Olive Schneider returned.

"Ready to order?" she asked.

"How was it to grow up here?" José probed.

"Slow but lovely; who wouldn't want to live in a medieval town perched on a hill with a real castle to boot? I knew the chatelaine when I was a kid; she was also our landlady, so I roamed amid armors and tapestries, kitchens with lines of copper pots hanging from oak crossbeams—some of them were gigantic. I ran up and down the stairwells to the many mysterious tower rooms that required large skeletons keys to unlock their doors. It was a magical town, José, but I fear it's all slowly going away."

"Such vibrant history that time robs us of, but we have much to look for ahead of us. A lot of it was so twisted and insanely brutal, that only the future can heal the damage done. It's where you, I, and our children come in, as well as those we help along the way. We're in charge of breaking the historical trauma that is responsible for perpetuating all that we deem evil, such as greed, inequality, and war."

"You almost make politics sound romantic; there must be a philosopher in you."

"Tragedy can be a mix of sweet and sour to those who don't have to deal with it directly. We romanticize evil to dehumanize the agony it engenders, so that we can call fools 'the brave,' and psychopaths 'leaders.'"

"Do you think any of this ties into what we're here to discuss today?"

"It might, Olive, but it all depends on whether we're on the same page or not."

"What about if I said, 'I need information on wrongdoings inside Child Protection Services and various orphanages around the country, with an emphasis on the greater area of Marseille'—would that put us in the same book?"

"I'd say we might even be on the same chapter."

"So what can you bring to the story, José?"

"I think I can warm up to you, Olive; maybe it's trust moving in... The brainchild I was referring to is an international réseau of safe houses for runaways and asylum seekers my wife and I, with the help of a few progressive thinkers, started out of Nancy and Metz a decade ago. It has no name, though some call us *the others*. I'm aware it's kind of a mythological item in the force, though it perplexes the mind that you guys can be so blind to it, considering how much some of your more zealous characters would want us dead if they knew we existed. But you know better than I do that the police are notorious for stepping all over themselves, hence the perpetual deriding. But I digress... It all began in Spain under the dictatorship of Motherfucker Franco. We became aware—meaning the party I belonged to—that many young exiles that had left for France fell under the radar. Most of them were the children of murdered parents. At first, we thought Franco was behind the disappearances, but our sources in Marseille, where most of the kids arrived by boat, dispelled the rumor—for once, the general was clean. So, in 1953, I crossed over to investigate. What I found was hard to get by, but I was lucky. It turned out that money was being funneled from the top down to finance operations of child prostitution, using methods spanning from abduction to deceitful rescue missions by bogus religious groups ironically tied to some church establishments, to snatch the kids. Additionally, there was a drug ring running the same waters, whose captains were seen hopping back and forth between 'cargos.' It was actually through them that I learned about the former. Opium was the big thing then, but heroin was on the rise, with most of the labs set in Marseille. The Sicilians were all over the map, but beyond *la Provence*, their footing in France was shaky. They needed a reliable route to Amsterdam which was known to supply the north continent, but they didn't care who controlled it, as long as they moved their merchandise and got their money. Marseille was essentially their wholesale market. They trusted neither the French nor the Arabs for very different reasons, but they didn't seem to mind dealing with Spaniards, probably because they thought we looked alike. That's where it got tricky."

"Don't tell me you took the job of running their drugs to Amsterdam," Schneider asked, looking stunned.

"Yes and no, although much later; all I did then was investigate the kids' disappearances."

"Do I need to get drunk to hear the rest?"

"Ordering another bottle may not be a bad idea!"

"Actually, I need to use the bathroom again, during which time I count on you to think of ways to not make me regret my decision to meet."

When Olive Schneider returned, the next course as well as a new bottle of St. Emilion had joined the table.

"Where were we?" she asked, avoiding José's eyes.

"As I said, we didn't start with the safe houses until the summer of 1959. By then, I had made quite a few contacts, both with the gangs in Marseille and the Federal Bureau of Narcotics, the latter in the process of implanting agents in Turkey and Southern France in response to heroin flooding the U.S. out of Marseille. You well know that this country doesn't have a Bureau of Narcotics of its own; instead, it relies on each police district to take care of its local drug problems. Consequently, opiates and cocaine can flow through France pretty much unimpeded, while cops pat themselves on the back busting users. But that's beyond the point... Olive, there is a limit to what I am permitted to divulge, but trust the income only serves to combat its source. At any rate, I believe that our common interest here isn't the narcotics. I think I have answered your original question; are we cool?"

"I see what you mean by trust having improved between us; that's quite a story, José! But what convinces you that I can be trusted with what you are telling me?"

"You're still not leveling with the field, Olive; it was your idea to meet and I assumed you meant what you said. In Spain, when parties have all to gain from each other, they forge alliances which have as much to do with the heart and dignity, as they have with logistics. But you're a cold gal from the grey north, cynical and conditioned to stay that way. Maybe you and I aren't destined to be allies."

"It's a bit of rash conclusion, Sir. I might be cautious—I'm a cop after all—but to go on saying I'm incapable of trust is somewhat unworldly."

"Don't you see my point though? I'm just as cautious as you are, that's why I'm not going to take you into the confidentiality of my work beyond the safe houses. I'm talking about bringing the shields down between us as humans, not jeopardizing other alliances or contracts."

"OK, maybe you're right about the northerner thing; we're just a cynical bunch. I guess I needed to hear it from you first in order to admit it. Now, I'm ready for an alliance."

The wine probably had a lot to do with it, but from the vantage of other tables in the room, Olive Schneider and José Perez looked like old friends having fun. A few regulars wondered briefly where the two were from, since tourist season was still a long way off, but it wasn't uncommon for merchants from Nancy, Metz, Brussels, or Strasbourg to frequent the Michelin-starred establishment. They soon blended in the comfort of privileged lifestyle.

"So, what are you up to, Olive? I don't assume it's your job at the station to snoop into Marseille's affairs."

"Alright... Bernie and I never had children of our own, so we adopted twin boys from an orphanage in

Toulon. They had just turned four. They wouldn't remember now, but at the time, they both lamented about their friends being taken away. We didn't think much of it then; after all, the orphanage was just a transitional place. But almost by accident, I came across data pertinent to the movement of orphans in and out of institutes. As it turned out, some of it showed disproportionate figures compared to other in similarly active metropolises. I was able to isolate those with the most blaring inconsistencies and access some of their records. What I found was stunning: case after case of systematic name whiteout, profuse corrections—or worse even—entire documents covering certain time periods simply gone missing. It was, as you're probably guessing, almost always consistent with the disappearance of the case subject. Incidentally, Julia Feraez's file is afflicted with comparable irregularities."

"Have you been able to trace these actions to agents or supervisors?"

"Mostly, the case worker's names shown on the files are either inconsequential or decoys aimed at shifting the blame. Those I'm interested in are never mentioned, so it helps to have police tools at one's disposal to cross-reference information such as, who's in charge of the precinct responsible for dealing with disappearance cases, or who the Mother Superior overseeing the orphanage is and whom she reports to. So, yes, I have names, activities, locations, and dates—it's a matter of putting things in order, mostly by connecting the dots."

"By adding my list of names to yours, I'm certain a lot more can be accomplished, but I want you to understand that the minute you step into the affairs of the men and women who build their fortunes by exploiting the misery of the underworld, your life will never be the same. For now, you're relatively safe in spite of having ruffled a few feathers, but if Vidal and/or the prefect have their hands dirty, it won't take much to uncover you without someone watching your back. In other words, you won't be able to work alone any longer. The main question is, are you willing to endanger the lives of your husband and children on top of your own?"

"Bernie knows what I'm doing. As a matter of fact, he's been able to provide me with information via what he calls, 'his sources.' Our children are presently studying in the States and living with his family."

"So, it's official; you and I are a team?"

"I'll be working on my trust issues, but yes, you can count on me. Before we leave, two things: is the kid from Fer with Julia? And, no, you don't have to go to Toul to warn your friend Johnny, because I left a message for him at work letting him know that his brother from Marseille is on his way to pick up his daughter. You see, I have my sources!" she said triumphantly.

"Impressive! As to your question, I guess you just want to hear what you already know from the mouth of the horse. In that case, yes—the two are madly in love."

18 – AREA MAPPING (Tue)

Superintendent Vidal's search confirmed what the CPS agents had said about Julia Feraez; she had no uncle in France. Whoever had taken her into their custody was a tool for something he didn't comprehend. Who would want her in the first place, unless it was the same people who had sheltered her since she escaped from the orphanage? The inside knowledge and the quick response was rather perplexing. For that, someone working at the precinct had to have provided that information. Additionally, the Jean-Michel Tourbé persona couldn't be living too far. It was just a matter of time before they would be apprehended, unless of course, the same person who leaked Feraez's arrest had already warned them.

Olive Schneider was certainly suspect, but it was too obvious, too much like a frame job to take hold. Many people worked at the station, so anyone could have spoken about the detainee. But to travel this fast while simultaneously reaching the right ears, the news required a particular set of circumstances, which, in Vidal's mind, excluded coincidence.

It all started with the kid from Fer. The cop began to sense there was something odd about him. It had been over a week since he went missing, yet he hadn't surfaced, which normally would call for a criminal investigation, but the parents hadn't pushed for a search, almost as if they had given up. But again, he was dealing with blue collars, whose kids often earned their own bread by the time they turned fourteen. Nonetheless, even though he couldn't prove there was a connection between him and the girl, he was almost certain there was one. It was a jumbled mess he couldn't make sense of, although it was clear there was a name to it, since the information Marseille needed had been hijacked by what appeared to be an organized group. The possibility of involvement by either the state or a foreign agency was a nagging concept Vidal couldn't ignore. One strategic mishap and his ass was on the line! Still, he felt it was his duty to find Julia Feraez and hand her over to CPS.

"Ernest, can you come over?" he called Jablonsky over the intercom.

The major entered and dragged a chair across the room to Vidal's desk.

"What's up, boss?" he asked.

"Schneider told me she had Feraez and Tourbé followed on Sunday; did you go over the report?"

"Yeah, they left Nancy and took off on Route 54."

"Any idea where they could have gone?"

"Assuming we can eliminate small towns and villages, Metz would be the farthest they went city-wise. But if they took the Mosel road the other way at the confluence of the Meurthe, they could have reconnected with the Paris-Strasbourg highway."

"We know we have to limit our search area to the larger periphery of Nancy. They probably knew they were being followed, so it's doubtful they took a straight line to their destination. We're looking for towns over ten thousand people, those most likely to include black residents," Vidal speculated.

"What about the *Tower Project*?"

"That would be our fucking luck, but I don't think it was Tourbé's idea to take his passenger to a war zone."

"Why didn't Schneider send an undercover after

them?" Jablonsky wondered.

"Because it was Sunday, that's why!"

"Don't we have some of our plainclothesmen working weekends?" the major insisted.

"Yeah, they were busy busting hippies at the train station," Vidal replied with pointed sarcasm.

There were over half a dozen towns of ten thousand inhabitants or more in the greater Nancy, and a few others in the Metz area. Vidal narrowed his search to the former, including Épinal, a city of thirty thousand in the Vosges. The idea was to start close and expand from there. The nearest three were Luneville, Pont-à-Mousson, and Toul, out of which, two were either on Route 54 or on the westbound off-branch along the Mosel, appropriately named *Toul Road*.

"The gendarmerie was notified yesterday; they'll be covering Toul and Pont-à-Mousson. But they have their own methods; by that I mean speed is not always factored in," Vidal told his right-hand.

"Did Schneider take the day off?"

"She left early for a doctor's appointment; she won't be back today."

"Do you really think she screwed up on Sunday, or was that just you having a moment?" Jablonsky asked.

"She acted irrationally, but what's new? At least she had the commonsense of having them followed."

"She was kinda caught between a rock and a hard place; perhaps irrationality had nothing to do with it. Though, it's true she could have told the fake uncle to come back the next day."

"That's exactly what I mean by irrational."

"What would you have done if you had been in her shoes'?"

"I would have made the right decision; that's what I would have done!"

"Why would you think she didn't; she's an officer after all. Are you insinuating only guys can make the right choices?"

"It's well known you have a crush on her, but if I were you, I would keep the heart out of it."

"You know, you can be a real asshole sometimes."

"Hey, you're on the job in case you forgot!"

"OK, boss, anything else you need from me?"

"You're in charge of Toul—see what you can dig up—I'll check the other towns. Remember to stay out of the other guys' hair; they take their turf seriously. Please, report to me by tomorrow night!"

19 – PLAINCLOTHESMAN (Tue)

The rain stopped shortly after Johnny had dropped the twins on his way to work. Julia put on her coat, kissed Stefan, crossed the yard between the barn and the main house, and told Suzanne she was going to take a walk downtown to check the stores. Besides the wish to get some fresh air and clear her mind, she wanted to surprise her lover with a small gift. She thought something with a musical theme would be appropriate; maybe there was a music store in town, or a bookstore that sold a few records as well. It would be nice to have something to play on the old Philips turntable in the barn.

It took a while before she reached the downtown area, which gave the rain the opportunity to return; but it was just a drizzle. She learned from a local that there was no proper record store in Toul, though just as she had intuited, there was a bookstore down the street that carried the more popular hit singles. The selection was dismal, but she found a copy of the Beatles' *Old Brown Shoe/The Ballad of John and Yoko*, paid for it, and left.

Few pedestrians dared the weather, but one of them, a short man in a beige trench coat, was seen walking ahead of her. Somehow, there was a familiar air to the way he nonchalantly went about his business. It took a mere second before the observation registered at the gut level. Julia stopped in her tracks to immediately take shelter in the doorway of a patisserie, just as Ernest Jablonsky turned around to inspect his surroundings. He then continued towards the end of the row of stores, briefly looking at window displays as if in search of ideas for a future purchase. She realized with mounting panic that the cop would be coming back her way before long. She couldn't afford to run or be seen walking ahead of him, her short afro being a clear giveaway. She had to hide in one of the stores until the man would pass, but the idea was abandoned upon realizing he could be walking into the same shop—none of them big enough to hide her from his trained eye. She came out of her retreat in a hurried pace, hoping to reach the first cross street before he would turn around. But no-one came after her as she spied from one of the deep doorways in the side alley. She waited. A minute later, Ernest Jablonsky ran by, trying to beat the icy rain that had just resumed falling. She would have to get wet after all, but there was comfort in the thought.

When Julia arrived at the house, Johnny was in the foyer, waiting anxiously. He had immediately taken off from work upon receiving the message that a woman had called about a mysterious uncle from Marseille coming for his guest.

"You have no idea how worried I was, girl. It appears there is a search going on and you can't be seen outside! Miss Schneider's superiors have probably caught up with the subterfuge, and it's possible she's the one who left the message."

"Well, little did we know that they would already be sniffing around; I almost ran into one of the two Nancy plainclothesmen that arrested me!"

"What in the world do you have that scares them to the point of them breaching protocol?"

"I'm not sure what protocol they operate under; what I know is that I'm gonna be eighteen soon and I won't have to hide anymore; which also means I will be free to tell my story."

"I'm gonna be blunt with you, baby girl: someone needs you to disappear before you have a chance to tell it—somebody with strings reaching deep into the system. Turning eighteen isn't going to make you safer!"

"But why me; I only have faces with no names?"

"They don't want you to meet the names without the faces; that's why."

"Heavy, man!"

"Anyway, go back in there and dry yourself by the woodstove; I'm sure Stefan has been missing you. Dinner at seven!"

Julia's idea of drying off was to take all of her clothes off and lie on her back on the rug in front of the stove. She had gifted Stefan with the record, which he immediately played on the cheap player. She reached for her bag and handed him a condom.

"It comes with the music, sweet boy," she said, while opening her legs to reveal the wetness of a no-longer containable arousal.

It was their first time having intercourse since they had fallen in love back at Jimmy's place, which explained why it took two additional condoms before they finally lay side by side, fully released from the shackles of having held back for so long.

"Thank you, Stef," Julia simply said.

"I'm the one who should thank you, Goddess."

"These are times I will never forget, regardless of what comes next; please, let's not say another word, dear one," she whispered, closing her eyes.

All sat at the kitchen table for dinner, following the twins' chasing ritual around the room.

"We'll take care of cleaning up; you, Johnny, and the boys can enjoy some time together in the living room by the fireplace," Julia offered, looking at Suzanne.

"You two are gems," the hostess expressed.

"Before we get too cozy, let's figure out the situation," Johnny said. "The presence of the Nancy plainclothes cop points to one thing: he's acting on specific orders from someone who doesn't want the locals to know what's going on. In other words—though it's technically not against the law—it's irregular. It also means that, whoever they may be, they are operating with a skeleton crew across a wide area. There is no doubt they are also looking in other cities. Julia identified Ernest Jablonsky, Superintendent Jean-Marie Vidal's henchman, as the guy who was spotted in town. He will come again until either he gets a lead or one is found elsewhere. I hope you understand the implications of what I'm saying... To hammer the point, Toul is no longer safe, unless you hole up in the barn until you, Julia, turn eighteen. But it doesn't mean it will end. Instead of cops on your tail, you'll have criminals; though I'm not at liberty to say where the line gets blurred. So, the pressing question is, 'How long are you willing to hide here?'"

"Since this whole thing started because of me, I think I'm in the right place to say that I don't see why we should endanger you. I can't speak for Julia, but I believe we ought to go somewhere far away from Nancy," Stefan said solemnly.

"I totally agree!" Julia voiced.

"Thank you for thinking about us, but you need to understand you're here because we chose it that way. We and José have been doing this for a long time; it's our life, our statement of responsibility towards a society that has failed its young as much as it has its elders. Don't ever think that you are imposing—we're here to help you because it is you they seek," Suzanne said.

"Nonetheless, I wouldn't want to witness you being wrong about this; I know where I came from and what they're capable of, and I'm sure you do as well, otherwise you wouldn't be talking about blurred lines between crime and the law," Julia said emphatically.

"Very well then, tomorrow we'll figure out the options—bon appétit!" Johnny said, somewhat perturbed.

20 – OLIVE & JOSÉ (Wed)

Olive Schneider had suspected José Perez of being involved in sheltering homeless children for quite some time. While the majority of the force had deemed the existence of such an organization to be the work of overactive imaginations, she saw the probability of it not as farfetched as her colleagues made it to be. But, runaways did not just consist of kids seeking to free themselves from the bonds of orphanages or dysfunctional families; she was well aware many had no home to go back to, especially if they originated from war countries. Those were the easy targets of predators, since the system rarely knew of their existence. While José had focused on the latter category, beginning with the disappearances of the Spanish children, Olive had concentrated her search on irregularities within the system. There too, lay the means of making a child vanish without arousing suspicion. It required a methodological approach to tampering with information and skillfully erasing tracks. The practice was in essence so simple that it led itself to invisibility; except when a deleted subject was caught in the crosshair of a new investigation, as in the case of an unknown relative appearing unexpectedly and asking hard questions. It was how Schneider came to suspect the possibility of joined corruption between state and religious institutions. She had no precise idea how deeply criminal organizations had infiltrated the system, but she could guess their influence was substantial.

On the other hand, José Perez was inside, working the drug routes side by side with those who had their hands in many pots. Besides the safe house network, which he ran like a private enterprise under the radar, his main job was tagging criminals for the Federal Bureau of Narcotics. In spite of his position, he lacked the powers to go after those involved in child exploitation and enslavement, and though he knew Olive Schneider had her hands tied, she was the closest to being a willing official as it came. There was nobody in the force he deemed trustworthy of not snooping in his affairs and making it an issue of legality, at the risk of opening the gates for criminals to step in and help themselves. It was essentially why it took so long for anything to move forward; distrust was at the base of it all. He could trust Olive, not that he believed she was fundamentally trustworthy, but because, as a woman, she lacked the leverage to engage the judicial machine into motion. Her male superiors would most likely, if reflexively, opt to defeat her over serving the law. It was his plan that by assisting her in exposing corruption inside the system— hoping it would lead to arrests and testimonies—her work would open the roof on organized crime and help the Bureau net the thugs. In other words, he needed someone to disable the tools put in place for the protection of criminals, from within the legal network. But though Schneider had both vital information and vantage, it was still to be determined how she would be able to persuade the force to go after its own bad guys. For that, she would have to work in the background, at making facts available at opportune times. José saw blessed irony in it, in that by working in the shadow, she would be a lot safer and free to maneuver without scrutiny. He needed Vidal, Muller, Sterns, and all the lowbrows of the central precinct to keep on seeing her as the token, obligatory female officer, displayed as a symbol of "male progressive action," empowered in her "female ways," but disengaged from blunt work and pivotal decisions.

José Felipe Perez was well aware he couldn't touch the church. The Vatican was a self-contained organization that dealt with its bad seeds with its own methods. No international law could breach the walls of its fortress, and no crime was high enough to merit exception. But he was confident that whatever the verdict and the means of punishment, a version of Hell would be the final destination.

Beyond the members of the Sicilian mafia and the 'Ndrangheta scouts involved in the European network, José was after what the Bureau referred to as the French Connection—a term that encompassed the activities of the Corsican clans responsible for the traffic of heroin into the U.S. via Canada. The problem was that they had been under the protection of the CIA and the French SDECE for the longest time, mostly to help them prevent the takeover of the old port of Marseille by communists. It was a curse made of multiple interests, overlapping in endless redundancies, which he was hoping the Bureau would help put an end to.

His meeting with Olive Schneider had shown promise; he felt he was ready to move forward in both his undertakings. At the core of it, he saw the arrest of the "fascist pigs" that leeched on the system, as well as the increased protection of homeless children, as a victory for communism ironically at odds with the socialist administration of Mayor Gaston Deferre, of Marseille.

But the lines of political ideologies were being blurred by corruptions borne of greed, private interests, and ineptitudes. In the end, it was about doing the right thing for those most likely to lack the tools of survival. José had seen the good and the bad thrive across the spectrum, he no longer needed a party to delineate which flavor of fanaticism, fatalism, or delusion he had a taste for. In his mind, he would always be a leftist, who, by far, favored action over rhetoric.

While José Perez had helped set up the drug route to Amsterdam, he was not running it. He supervised its operation and advised on better methods of concealment and distribution. But, what had began as a temporary assignment, had turned into a long-term project, in which he started likening himself to being another cog in a nefarious scheme, as some of the drugs had made their way into the safe houses. But the Bureau had advised on patience as it prepared for action, and so, the Spaniard saw in it an opportunity to concentrate more on the child trafficking side, and keep a tab on the operators most likely to cross over. He was hoping to kill two birds with one stone, or at least inflict damage on the second one, pending Vidal's secretary's full involvement.

Olive Schneider entered the names of the two CPS agents who had come for Julia, into a file that she named *Marseille papers*. Although she had no intention of making it personal, agent Francis Visconti's innuendo—

upon him leaving the office—was enough to fuel the embers of suspicion. Time would tell whether he and agent Monique Colbert played instrumental roles in doctoring Julia Feraez's file or not. In the meantime she needed to find a way to protect herself in case they tried to dig up dirt on her.

She called various departments to obtain the lists of past and present CPS case managers and branch directors, to evaluate their relationships with the *Police Nationale*, orphanages, and foster care services. The job was to establish links between her results and the names provided by José Perez. She had dedicated an entire wall of her home office to the mapping of these connections, with the suspects circled in red. Among them were Superintendent Vidal, Marseille police chief—Erik Schmitt, the head nun overseeing the *Côte d'Azur* area orphanages—Sister Daniela Graziano, the archbishop of Marseille, the bishop of Ajaccio, as well as the heads of CPS Provence. But Schneider knew were to draw the line; "suspect" didn't mean "guilty," even if the modus operandi of the French justice was to reverse-engineer guilt into innocence. She had no case and no evidence, not even the power to convince someone in the force to open one for her. It would take time before she got to that point. For now, the job was to complete the map and define the collusive patterns between its elements.

21 – TWENTY-ONE (Wed)

Julia and Stefan got up early to meet with Johnny and Suzanne about moving out of Toul. The logistics were ill-defined, mostly due to the lack of preparedness and last second developments.

"I want to make sure that you two understand the complications of lodging runaways. Safe houses are not like a hotel chain; they rely on the willingness of simple folks to accommodate what often sums up to be difficult teens. In a nutshell, we don't appreciate being taken for granted. That is why I want the four of us to think about it long and wide, so that we can come up with mutually agreeable solutions," Johnny explained.

"You know I would never take you for granted, Johnny, and sorry if I make it sound like I don't see what you guys put into helping us. Actually, it's more like I don't know how to make it up to you. I just don't want to take advantage, and I'm sure Stefan feels the same," Julia returned.

"Thanks, I just had to say my bit. As far as Suzanne and I are concerned, you're cool until further notice, as long as you understand you have to stay in for a while."

"But we can still talk about options, can't we?" Stefan inquired.

"Absolutely, my man; I just have to speak with José. Keep in mind our phone lines are far from secure, so I'll have to drive to Nancy to connect. I'm fairly certain Strasbourg and Paris have openings; those would be your two closest options. Of course, since you, Julia, want to return to Marseille, it would only be temporary."

"That wouldn't be the first time. Actually, I don't think anything was ever permanent in my life!" Julia replied.

"I misspoke," Johnny returned, smiling.

"Considering the situation, I don't think it's wise for Julia to return to Marseille. I mean, don't they want her dead down there? What's your take on it Johnny?" Stefan asked.

"I agree, but you apparently don't know how stubborn Miss Julia can be. The danger will be just as great then as it is now. The thing is the legal age is actually twenty one, but France recognizes eighteen as the mark at which one can fend for themselves, providing the parents agree. So, technically, CPS could still have an influence."

"Fuck that!" Julia spat.

"You will have legal rights, nonetheless, and no-one should question your travels," Johnny said, aiming at reassuring her.

"I've been waiting like forever to get in position to look for my brother—CPS ain't gonna mess that up for me. It's not because José couldn't find him that I won't!"

"You still have a couple of months to get prepared for it, and we might be able to assist you with more information; there have been some developments which might provide us with an inside picture—I'll explain later."

"Were you able to speak with José since what happened yesterday?"

"Not José, but Jimmy came by after you two retired to the barn. He told me we had made contact with someone in the force who could prove invaluable in assisting us locate missing individuals."

"Does it mean it might be possible for me not to go to Marseille?"

"Yes, especially if your brother is elsewhere."

"'Elsewhere' is where I'm going then!"

"We can't promise anything, the least of it being where your brother might be at; meaning, caution is still de rigueur, Miss Julia."

"I'll be the judge of that when we meet again!" she dropped.

"Very well then; I'll keep you two posted on what José and I come up with. I have a half day off, so I'm on my way to the city. Catch ya later!"

"How absurd is that? I mean, you can drink alcohol legally at sixteen, but you can't take a piss without your parents' authorization," Stefan said.

"Don't ever become one of them, Stef; I would lose my respect for you."

"By them, I assume you don't mean José, Suzanne, Johnny, Jimmy, and *the others*, because I wouldn't mind becoming one of them."

"Then I would love you more!" she laughed.

"If you didn't have to look for your brother, and you and I could go anywhere we wished; which place would you choose?"

"San Francisco, in a heartbeat!"

"Wow, somehow I didn't expect you'd pick a U.S. city, but what a great choice—I'd love to live there too!"

"Maybe my brother's already there..."

"Wouldn't that be perfect!"

"Why would you want to live there, Stef?"

"Because some of my favorite bands are in the States. Last summer, while I was on vacation in the country with my folks, I befriended a hitchhiker from Michigan. It turned out he was roommates with Jimmy Osterberg of the Stooges in Ann Arbor. His step dad's Jerry Lee Lewis; he showed me pictures of him and Jerry Lee in Memphis—isn't that wild?"

"You mean the rocker who plays the piano like a madman?"

"Yup, that guy!"

"The more I know you, the more there is to know; you think you'll see him again one day, you know, the hitchhiker?"

"I dunno, maybe... He was on his way to Turkey. I told him the place was known to be dangerous outside Istanbul."

"And how did you know that?"

"Cuz I thought of going to India, so I investigated among the people who'd returned from there. They said Turkey and Iran were hellholes where the beating, rape, and even murder of hippies occurred all the time."

"Shit, that's crazy! Can we go to India after I find my brother, but not through those places?"

"I thought you wanted to go to San Francisco?"

"Maybe, from India, we can go there!"

22 – SCHMITT & VISCONTI (Thu)

Francis Visconti closed the CPS report. He was left with figuring out how to explain why Feraez had slipped between his fingers. Erik Schmitt had insisted on a no margin of error transfer; meaning the girl was precious cargo. He understood she was instrumental in the process of solving a "sensitive case," but it remained unclear as to what it was. As usual, he would be kept in the dark, which he didn't mind in most instances, but this time around, there was no money because of the failure to bring her back, even though technically, he and Colbert weren't the reason for it. He resented both the Marseille chief of police and the female cop from Nancy for the situation, so the best he could do to assuage that feeling, was to pit the two against each other. He had done it before under similar circumstances, taking great satisfaction in the ensuing damage.

"So, what happened up there?" Schmitt asked.

"The gal was gone by the time your friend Vidal took us to the department."

"Yes, I already know that, since I spoke with him. But my question still stands—so...?"

"So, that's it; we took the train back."

"I didn't ask if nothing happened, did I?"

"What do you want me to say?"

"I want you to tell me what you did to compensate for the fact someone snatched her from underneath you. What kinds of questions did you ask Vidal's secretary besides threatening her pointlessly? I know her too well, for having been her boss, to rest assured your remark didn't go unnoticed. It is for Vidal to rectify the errors of his team as he sees fit—he's fully capable of that. So, if he deems Olive Schneider acted in line with the authority of her rank, it isn't your job to threaten an investigation into the reasons of her choice. What you actually did, was jeopardize the cover of the case; now, she's probably wondering what was so important about getting the girl back, and I wouldn't be surprised if she sought to investigate CPS' motives."

"And how by asking the right questions wouldn't I have jeopardized the cover of the case?"

"By politely requiring going over the facts one by one, so that your report would look less like hers, and more like yours. Does it not make sense to you?"

"And how would that have changed anything? The girl was gone!"

"Maybe you could have waited a bit longer instead of calling from the Lyon train station to tell me you were already on your way back. Your extended presence could have helped towards locating the kid before her tracks fully disappeared. Ever heard of silent persuasion?"

"I'm not a cop."

"I always thought you wanted to be one, that's why I trusted you," Schmitt said.

"At any rate, I don't believe you called me in here just to lecture me. I'm sure you're dying to know why I said what I said to the secretary," Visconti countered.

"Was she lying?"

"I believe she was."

"I don't need proofs, but substance would be nice; how do you think she lied?"

"My take is that she arranged to be at the station

on her day off to help facilitate the release."

"So, you're saying that she spoke with Tourbé beforehand, am I correct?"

"It kinda jumped at me."

"Which would indicate she might have been working for someone outside the force, unless she wanted the help the girl, because her husband's also black?"

"That would hardly explain the fake uncle; she didn't have enough time to introduce another player of her own."

"Therefore she knew how bad we wanted the girl; is that your take, Visconti?"

"By how bad she didn't want us to get to her, I'd say yes."

"You understand this is just between us; I'm not inculpating Olive Schneider. As far as I know, we can't prove any of it and there's no valid reason to question her actions. I was just seeking an opinion. I'll let you and Colbert know when we locate Feraez. Rule of thumb: never threaten a person of the force. Have a good day!"

Visconti understood why the police chief was making light of Schneider's interference, but it was none of his business what would happen next; the dice had been rolled. It was just another one of those internal affairs in which he and Monique Colbert were mere operators. CPS didn't care one way or the other; they were mostly an instrument of the force in dealing with delinquents and bridging the gap to Juvenile Hall. As far as they were concerned, Julia Feraez had been missing for too long to matter and was now old enough to take care of herself. Whatever the *Police Nationale* did with her was none of their business. The report he and Colbert had filed with the department didn't even include her name; it was a mere expense breakdown for a misscheduled trip only relevant to accounting.

But what was nagging at the gates of Francis Visconti's ability to think clearly was the possibility he was unknowingly working for something larger than the police department. The question had only minimally arisen while he was being adequately remunerated, but the affront of having been stiffed this time around, had washed away the opacity from always having looked the other way. Perhaps now was the time to call Nancy.

Olive Schneider picked up the phone. It was from a male case manager at CPS, requesting verification of the visit of two of their agents.

"Yes, they came here on Monday, but they were too late."

"Too late for what?" the voice asked.

"You mean you don't know?"

"Police Chief Erik Schmitt didn't brief us on the reasons he requested two agents to be sent your way. But as far as we know it was in error. I'm just calling to finalize expenses for the trip, so that accounting can do their job."

"Very well then, may I have your name?"

"Yes, Mario Oliveira. Sorry to bother you; I just wanted to make sure—thank you and God bless!"

23 – THE OFFICE (Thu)

Olive Schneider paused to gather her thoughts. Did she hear correctly that CPS wasn't looking for Julia Feraez, but only Erik Schmitt was? That was an interesting development. So, who was Francis Visconti, and what power did he have to question her decision? Obviously, if he wasn't representing CPS, who was he speaking for? Up to that point, she thought the agent to be an overzealous case manager, but she was mistaken. As a matter of fact, he made the critical error of threatening her, leading to exposing Erik Schmitt as the sole reason Julia was to return to Marseille, and possibly incriminating him in a case of malfeasance. She knew from Vidal that the girl was pivotal to a critical case, but as far as José was concerned it was bullshit, which had left CPS as the primary bad guy. It was now becoming clear the agency was being used by the Marseille police through puppets in its system, like Visconti and Colbert.

Olive picked up the phone. She needed to ascertain Mario Oliveira was really who he claimed he was. The operator switched her to his desk. His phone rang three times before he picked-up.

"Mario Oliveira, Child Protection, how may I help you?"

"Olive Schneider, Nancy police, I forgot to ask for the case number for my records."

"There isn't one. As I said, it was a mistake—sorry."

"Thanks, I'll just enter *no number* in my report."

She hung up the phone. Francis Visconti did the

115

same at the other end then returned to his desk. He and Oliveira, who was off for the day, shared the same office. The game was on. It didn't matter whether she could dig dirt on him or not; as far as he was concerned, he was just an employee of CPS who followed orders. The only individuals capable of hurting him couldn't afford the spotlight.

Olive Schneider was familiar with Erik Schmitt's methods. She had worked under him for nearly ten years. He was ambitious, intellectually gifted, and ruthlessly competitive. He had shaped Jean-Marie Vidal in his mold and the two had remained good friends after the Marseille promotion. It was one of the main reasons why the superintendent often—though, in vain—pitted his department against the one of his tutor. While Marseille was the number one crime city in Europe, Nancy was merely the unhappiest place to live in the country, which put Vidal at a serious disadvantage.

Olive needed to connect with José, but they hadn't spoken about how to meet incognito yet. She lived on Hill Street, close to downtown; she would swing by Le Thiers in the evening, just in case he would be seeing some people there. Lunch in the company of the Spaniard in Liverdun had left her with a heightened sense of belonging, but the feeling had quickly dwindled into mild frustration from the momentary void of incapacitation. The call from Oliveira carried the potential of a lead into what Schmitt and, maybe, Vidal were up to; something that involved Julia, and which could put the girl in harm's way. She didn't mind being wrong; she just couldn't bear sitting on information that could possibly help save someone's life if it were allowed to flow. She realized it was nearly the end of her shift; it was time to put order into her day's work.

José Perez was ready to leave *Le Thiers* when he spotted Schneider. She was at the bar sipping an Irish coffee, checking the large expanse of mirrors to ascertain no-one from the department was present. The Spaniard squeezed by her and bought a pack of *Gauloises* from the bartender.

"Meet me outside the train station by the taxi line; I'll be parked there," he said in a low voice and left.

Olive Schneider calmly finished her drink, got up while adjusting her hair, then walked towards the washrooms and the rear exit. She avoided crossing the plaza; instead, she went around it, passing the main newspaper building where typesetters could be seen aligning sorts in composing sticks. She spotted José's 2CV at the pick-up zone, used a side entrance into the main hall, checked the large schedule board, and left through the main portal to connect with her ride.

"I saw your elaborate path; do you think you're being followed?" the driver asked.

"I don't trust Vidal. I'm glad you got the innuendo of my presence back there."

"I figured you were trying to get my attention," José returned, as he pulled out of the line.

"Where are you taking me?"

"I share an office space above a car dealership in *Laxou*—no-one's ever around at this time. It's a safe place to meet and operate from. I had copies of the keys made for you."

Minutes later, the Citroën found its way into an underground lot, whence the two reached *the office* via an iron service stairwell. The imposing, solid oak door into the space inspired confidence. The room was unexpectedly large and tall, more like an old, wood-paneled classroom than the cramped place that she had imagined. There were three desks close to each other in a line, facing windows overlooking the avenue, each with a typewriter, a rolodex, a lamp, and a phone.

"It may seem strange to work with your back to the door, but we don't normally have visitors, so why not enjoy the daylight! You may not see it in low light, but the trees are tall enough to hide us from the building across the street; that is, when they have leaves, of course," José said humorously.

"Who are you sharing this with?"

"You will meet them in time. For now, let's get you familiarized with the setup. First of all, we have three unlisted phone lines that technically don't exist at the level of your department, which naturally means they can't easily be tapped. All the calls pertaining to your research should, from now on, be made from one of them. I will arrange to have an extra desk brought in, so that in the rare instance of all of us being here together, you won't have to work on the floor. We have plenty of extra filing space; therefore I recommend you move all of what you have at home in here—no need to compromise your private life by having snoopers find out what you've been up to. If you're careful, nobody will ever know you come here; we're the only ones who use the underground parking and the service stairs—they're part of the rental."

"What are you operating under, I mean, what's your cover?"

"The best cover is no cover—unlisted numbers, remember? The landlord is a U.S. real estate company whose address is a room in an unmarked building located in an undisclosed American city."

"I see how Vidal might break his teeth on this one. I'm impressed, Sir," Olive said, somewhat dazzled.

"You just gonna have to keep this away from your husband, until we can determine whether he can be trusted or not. I'm sure you have no objection?"

"Of course, Bernie doesn't need to know. He's aware he married a cop; we don't ask the wrong questions between us."

"That makes for a healthy relationship. I wish it were more the norm than the exception," José remarked.

"OK, so what else do I need to know?"

"The teleprinter will come in handy as soon as you establish your contacts; you'll even be able to send or forward texts from your office at the police department to it, without giving us or yourself away. I'm not well versed in technology, but supposedly, some encoding makes it invisible. Then the usual suspects: photocopier, Nagra recorder tied to the lines, coffee maker, mini-fridge, and a small liquor cabinet, integral to the shelving unit, that comes in handy on occasion."

"Once again, you don't disappoint, José. I'll start bringing my stuff over this weekend, if it's OK."

"That'll be fine. Now, let's get to what brought us here in the first place. I assume you have news."

"Yep, CPS weren't the ones looking for Julia; it was solely an Erik Schmitt decision to bring her back to Marseille. I spoke with one of their agents, who had no idea who Julia Feraez was. According to him, Colbert and Visconti traveled on a request from Police Headquarters, but as it turned out, there was miscommunication between offices and the case was annulled. I couldn't even get an ID number out of him."

"Didn't one of them threatened to investigate your decision?"

"You're catching up quickly. Yes, and why would he do that if he wasn't supposed to know who our detainee was? Visconti and Colbert weren't working for CPS, but Schmitt, rather. So, I need to figure out what these two are up to. As far as I know, they are indeed case managers there."

"That is if CPS are telling the truth. But let's say they are; that leaves us with two rogue managers serving double duty, one of them to provide potentially confidential information about their clients to parties that may have questionable motives for requesting that info."

"We don't even need to verify Visconti's status, he already gave himself away by threatening me. During the time I trusted he represented Child Protection, I didn't think his comment was more than another pathetic display of male authority, but if CPS have nothing to do with it, we can assume he's a mole of the police."

"A pertinent assumption worth of consideration. I think you may have to make a list of all the other case managers suspected of betraying their clients; that could help define the surface area at the base of the pyramid."

"Alongside figuring out why Schmitt wants Julia down there," Olive added.

"Which brings us to upping her protection; we might have to transfer her and Stefan to a safer location, since Jablonsky was seen 'window-shopping' in Toul."

"Of course, the whole CPS thing brings suspicion down on *The Couple*'s motives behind their search for Julia. It is becoming more and more obvious they have become tools of Marseille."

"Based on what I know, I don't think Schmitt is the mastermind behind wanting our protégée. The whole thing is a Pandora's Jar full of bad characters, whose names are in dire need of protection. The cultural revolution of the sixties has been bad to those assholes. As a whole, people think differently than they did back in the day—they are now starting to take charge of their reality," José Perez concluded.

24 – THE CORSICAN (Fri-Sat)

Superintendent Erik Schmitt hung up the phone following his conversation with Chief Superintendent Joseph Pinelli, his superior, and the man he reported to on affairs concerning the runaways who had fled orphanages and foster families. It did not go well. He rang his friend Vidal to remind him that tremendous pressures were being applied from the top to locate Julia Feraez at all cost.

"The end justifies the means, Jean-Marie; you know that from training, and you've also been taught on how to erase the tracks—whatever it takes," Schmitt said in disquieting tones.

"You're asking me to find a needle in a haystack, Erik, on top of not having a team."

"Listen, here we find Negros in a town full of them; don't tell me you can't find one in a white town. As to a team, put one together! Get your guys to pull their heads out of their own asses, you're not running a nursery!"

Vidal had been at the blunt end of Schmitt's anger before; the last thing he needed was to piss him off for not delivering. He would never have made it to superintendent without his tutor's unending patience and influence in the field. He owed Schmitt the decency to do his best when asked for a favor.

"I'll report when we have her," he countered.

"Make it quick and don't hesitate to off the motherfuckers that come in your way; we'll ask the questions later. All we care about is the chick. Can I count on you to make this right, Jean-Marie?"

"Yes, Sir, as I said, I'm on it!"

"Good boy—talk soon!"

Rather than drive, Schmitt decided to walk the length of the *Canebière* to meet with the Corsican at a café by the old port. Even though Vidal had promised to do his best, he knew he couldn't deliver—not gutsy enough, and prone to sentimentality. And neither could he count on the CPS case agents, because they were compromised as the result of Visconti's ego running at the mouth and threatening Schneider. As to Olive, she could never be bought; hence, she presented an obstacle that might prove insurmountable to Vidal. Actually, she was the only one with a spine in the department when he ran it—he appreciated that in her. For that reason, she was the one to watch.

The Corsican was an all-purpose go-to-guy who was known for finishing what he started, and generally—cleanly. Schmitt had decided that sending him to Nancy was his better chance of getting the girl. The man from the *Island of Beauty*, as Corsica was known, had a visceral distaste for obstacles and could apply the appropriate methods to make them disappear. He also had an uncanny ability to find his targets with just one look at a picture and an approximate location. He also detested cops, especially those from Marseille, whom he referred to as continental swine. But Schmitt wasn't acting in his capacity as the chief of police, and that was good enough for the Corsican who kept to one side of the line. For a fee, he would be back with the girl in a matter of days.

Missing the deadline on delivering the girl had sent ripples into areas Schmitt didn't enjoy frequenting. Joseph Pinelli had insisted he reassured Mother Graziano, who had been worried sick about the teen's wellbeing since her disappearance nearly four years prior. He abhorred the church as much as the Corsican hated continental cops, having been raised amid the carnage of a corrupt faith, as he described it. The fact that Schmitt was born in Protestant Alsace, was of little consequence to him—he was a rigid atheist, who saw organized religion as a tool to stifle human evolution by keeping its subjects in a perpetual state of imbecilic stupor.

He met with the nun in her office. The smell of old cedar and frankincense, combined with the sight of crosses and statues of the Blessed Virgin were enough to bring him to the edge of nausea. Daniela Graziano was old, and like most nuns her age, a few rebellious bristles protruded from her chin as if designed to draw the listener's attention to that part of her face. But her main features were her eyes, dark as coals, icy, and penetrating.

"You understand she is still a child of the state, and thus belongs here with us until she comes of age, Superintendent. We rely on God's servants such as yourself to bring the lamb back to the sheepfold. I heard through the channels that your men let her slip through their fingers; how was that allowed? Never mind, I don't even want to know. Let me make it clear, my child: humble servants and generous benefactors of Mary, Mother of Jesus, have prayed daily for her return. I would hate to disappoint them with the news of your failure. They are prepared to cover all necessary expenses, as well as triple your usual fee for the safe return of our Julia. I believe you should find the offer quite agreeable."

"A new team is on it, Sister Daniela; it's only a matter of days."

"Then all has been righted under God's light, Superintendent. Don't forget to stop by the font on your way out."

The Corsican exited the Nancy train station, walking straight to the taxi line. He inspected the drivers and settled on the eldest of them.

"How long have you been driving cabs in this town?" he asked.

"Over thirty years—my own business—why?"

"I'll let you know when you get to the front of the line—I'll be there."

"That doesn't guarantee someone won't get to me first."

The Corsican smiled and gave the driver a loose two-finger salute before strolling towards the head cab. He looked at the large station clock; it was nine—he had traveled all night. He unfolded the morning paper purchased from the kiosk, first checking the obituary page as he always did. Stefan Vogt's picture sat across from it in the notification section. He refolded the paper, tucked it inside his bomber jacket and stepped into the cab that had just pulled up.

"You see!" he told the driver.

"You had it all planned out—where to?"

"How much time before your lunch?"

"Three hours, maybe four depending on business."

"Four it is, then!"

The Corsican took two hundred francs out of a roll

of hundreds, handing the money to the cabby.

"Take me where your blacks live, and every single place you remember seeing one—no questions. In the meantime, we can chat about the life and such if you need to talk."

"We'll start with the *Tower Project*; it's where most of them live; then we can take it from there. You're from Marseille?"

"Cervione, Corsica—ever been down there?"

"My wife and I visited Ajaccio before the war. We boated at Marseille, but halfway through the voyage, we were hit by a massive storm. My wife thought we were gonna die—a lot of puking going around."

"Beauty doesn't come without pain, but sorry we made it hard on you," the Corsican humored.

The cab crawled through the project as the passenger looked out absentmindedly. He asked to go around a few times before declaring he had seen enough.

"There's a black teenager that hangs out around Old Town, OK going there?"

"As I said, wherever you've seen blacks."

"I guess we'll inspect the suburbs next."

No blacks were spotted in Old Town. The Corsican wanted to be driven around the downtown area for a while, to get familiarized with the city ahead of hitting the suburbs. He also asked they stop by the main precinct for a minute. A big part of his work was mapping; finding the straight lines from those that zigzagged or looped, as well as defining strike zones and escape routes. He was efficient at it, a product of his exceptional photographic memory and his finely calibrated inner compass. That was why he was in high demand.

The driver, who had been absorbed by his own

thinking after deducing his client wasn't known for his conversational skills, suddenly came alive.

"It's funny, but that just came back to me. A couple of days ago, a client who had missed his last train and bus connections to Toul, was talking about how there was only one black man in town, and then this girl showed up; and just like that, there were two. Then he said, 'Next they'll be three and four, until France becomes theirs.' He was a nut, but since you're looking for blacks, I thought you might be interested. I've never seen blacks in Toul myself."

"The Oracle of Delphi once said, 'Look under every stone.' That's our job today. What's your name, by the way?"

"Emile, Emile Dollinger, and yours?"

"You can call me the Corsican, though my first name's Sergio, Sergio the Corsican. I guess all you people have kraut names in these parts."

"Not all, but a bunch; it doesn't mean we fought for the Germans."

"As long as you didn't fight for the Ruskies, I don't care who you fought for."

"Before we go to the suburbs, d'you mind stopping for lunch; I'm famished?"

"Fair enough, you can drop me on *Place Carrière*—no need to wait. How much do I owe you?"

"You've already paid for it; actually I'm the one who owes you."

"Nah, here's another fifty. Enjoy your lunch!"

The Corsican thought it would be a good idea to take an easy stroll around Old Town while the rain was holding off. Something told his senses that there were still fresh tracks on the old cobblestones. There was plenty of time for him to investigate before catching a bus for Toul.

One of the things that made the Corsican special in his line of work was extraction through deceit teamed to confusion. So after he ate his cheese sandwich and drank two espressos, he was ready for action. By the time he found himself by the record store behind St. Epvre church, he knew he had found his strike zone.

He remembered the name and the face of the kid in the newspaper; there was the very remote chance runaways knew of other runaways and that others knew them as well.

"Hey, aren't you a friend of Julia's—Stefan told me she moved to Toul?!" he asked, accosting one of the customers coming out the store.

"Who's Julia?"

"Sorry, my mistake!"

And so it went until the Corsican inconspicuously bumped into a lankly, stoned-looking, bearded hippie carrying a guitar—same question.

"How do you know Stefan?" Jimmy answered, not fully realizing he had been set up.

"Friend of the family."

"Probably a different Stefan, sorry man!"

It was too late; Sergio had all he needed. He followed Jimmy to the studio, and before the main gate had a chance to close behind the musician, Jimmy was spun around to find himself face to face with the Corsican holding a knife to his throat.

"Take me slowly to your pad—no squealing or you're dead—got it?"

They got inside.

"Where's your stash?" the Corsican demanded.

"I don't keep money in here."

"Do I look like someone who needs money? I'm asking for your drugs, shithead!"

"Behind the record stacks," a panicked Jimmy mumbled.

"Ha, it looks like you're into shooting, boy," the hitman grimaced, emptying a small bag of heroin into a glass that he filled with tap water, stirring.

"Now, you drink that or I cut your throat—your choice."

While Jimmy was convulsing on the floor, the Corsican sniffed around the room for artifacts that might prove Julia Feraez once lived there. He found it in a Polaroid shot of her and Stefan Vogt taken in the studio.

Sergio locked the door behind him, pocketed the keys, and briskly left the building.

25 – THE BARN (Sat)

It was unusual for the Corsican to get sloppy, but perhaps because Jimmy lived in such a small apartment building, barely larger than a big house, he didn't suspect a concierge to be lurking from behind the fisheye door viewer of her flat when he entered and left. She immediately called the police, who broke into the tenant's space and called an ambulance. Jimmy survived.

The news promptly traveled to Olive Schneider's emergency home line. Since she was in the process of consolidating the things she needed to bring to *the office* she now shared with José, she drove there straightaway to call the Spaniard from the safe phone. José was there within minutes. He was unable to reach Johnny and Suzanne who could have been taking the twins out for the afternoon. Based on the time of Jimmy's rescue, the perpetrator couldn't have gone too far. In the worse case scenario, he would be on his way to Toul in his own vehicle or a taxi, but it was unlikely the studio gave away Johnny's address. They still had a chance to get there first.

"Olive, you have the faster car, let's hit the road; we have no time to waste!"

José opened the safe and pulled out a holster nesting a Colt M1911 pistol.

"I have a firearm in the DS as well, you're sure we can't involve the Police or the Gendarmerie?"

"That would be messy, plus they'll know soon enough; we'll let them deal with the mop-up."

"If Vidal only knew what I have gotten into..."

"It'd be you that'd need saving!" José cut.

Olive was a skilled driver, who piloted a fast and nimble car. They reached Johnny and Suzanne's place in record time, but not before the Corsican had already figured out where Julia and Stefan were holed up. By then, he was already crossing the small courtyard between the main house and the barn. He kicked the door in to find Julia sitting in the middle of the room and Stefan, with his guitar, leaning against the back wall. He leaped towards the boy with the snap of his OTF auto knife, but Julia tripped him, making him lose his balance and fall, his head slamming against one of the oak posts. By the time he got up, José's gun was pressed against his temple and Olive had kicked his wrist with such force that the knife flew across the room to plant itself in the wall plaster. Within seconds, the Corsican was on his knees in handcuffs.

"You two go in the house!" José ordered Julia and Stefan.

"You should have seen how she tripped that asshole!" Stefan uttered in a quivering tone.

"We'll go over the details later; for now, we need to conduct business with this gentleman.

"I know him," Julia said.

"How do you know him?" Olive asked.

"He's friends with the father of the teenagers that raped me when I was twelve. His name's Sergio; he's from Corsica."

"I know who he is too, but we've never met. We'll talk later, sweetie—please, go to the house just in case the rightful renters return. We don't want them to come in here," José said.

"I don't think this guy will talk," Olive said.

"It all depends on the methods."

"What do you mean?"

"I learned from General Franco that everyone eventually tells their story."

"And you think here is the right place?"

"You haven't seen the rest of the barn yet."

"So, d'you have a name, besides Sergio?" José asked the man with his arms tied around a post.

"Fuck off!"

"Sergio Fuckoff, that sounds Russian; but that would be Sergei then, Sergei Fuckoff, correct?"

"Oh brother, a Corsican communist, I thought I had heard it all," Schneider chimed in.

"If you think I'm gonna talk, you must be fools!"

"You already couldn't help giving up your name; so we're on a good start." Olive countered.

"You see, Sergei, the thing is we don't need to hear you talk, 'cause we already know all there is to know about you. No, it's us that will talk, so that you can listen and hear firsthand how we're going to fuck the whole deal for you, the continental swine from Marseille, the bitch Graziano, and your family of heroin smugglers out of Corsica. You see, Fuckoff, I know where you come from, the stone houses, the chestnut trees, the wild pigs, the bootlegged tobacco and the booze, the wild parties at night, shooting guns and letting your children drink into a stupor. I was there, so I know what you breathe, eat, and shit. I know when you take your siesta and later reopen your stores. Life is simple where you're from, man. Here, it's a lot more complicated, and that's why you got sloppy—it's the German curse. Anyway, you may not talk, but even if you pretend to not listen, you can't unhear. It's automatic, the brain can't help it, especially with your kind of photographic memory, everything is recorded in that skull of yours and nothing ever gets erased," José pressed.

"I curse your family, shithead!"

"Too late, Franco took care of that. There isn't much that can touch me and what is left of my kin. So curse away, choirboy!"

"We know who you work for, the Schmitts, the Pinellis; the individuals and the families that keep the orphanages ticking like Swiss clocks with their large donations, so that innocent children can flow to their horrific fates, and heroin can reach the shores of America," Olive Schneider warned.

"You know nothing, bitch!"

"Sorry, wrong answer, and quite typical for your kind. You see, you keep on talking, even though you threaten to bore us with silence. You're a real chatterbox, Sergio!" Olive bounced back.

The Corsican looked apoplectic. José was deeply impressed by Olive's eloquence; the woman had obvious experience handling hardened criminals. He turned to the prisoner.

"You must know by now that you're not dealing with your average law and order. You're used to operating around cops that aren't smart enough to catch up with your shenanigans, so you can afford to get soft, even sloppy. I mean, man, you left that poor kid foaming at the mouth for dead, but he ain't dead. You're used to cops who work for you, but here, in Germany, as your ill-kind so affectionately refer to this part of France, we

133

don't get bought and owned by the mob. The few that try, we let them play until they deliver the bad guys to us. You come here to shit on our turf—you fucking lose! All that to say this is war. There are two options for you: either we off you here and now or we send you back with a message; or maybe, as a third option, we can send you back, dead, with a message. That's what the Sicilians would do, and I know the Sicilians even better than I know the Corsicans. But let's pretend we're German; what would a German do, Fuckoff? I'll tell you what a German would do, he would send you back with a medal for most fucked up assignment and let the powers that be deal with the consequences. But you wouldn't know about psychology – too complicated for a mountain man who was raised amid wild boar."

"Die, Spanish whore!"

"Hey, bravo, you finally got I was from Spain! How many 'Francos' did it take? You're going back to Marseille, fucker; I'll make personally sure that you get to tell your story to Schmitt. Let's haul his ass away! Wait, he needs to piss first; I wouldn't want him to soil the car, partner. Who's holding his dick?"

"That would be a job for *The Couple*. Let it hang, he can piss on his shoes!" Olive Schneider returned.

While José kept an eye on the Corsican in the back barn, Olive went to the main house to speak with Julia and Stefan,

"Not a word to Suzanne and Johnny—we don't need to freak them out. Please clean up the mess, we'll be back tomorrow. For now, you're out of harm's way, but things could heat up in a hurry in the next couple of weeks, so hold tight and keep on loving each other; there's not enough of that in the world—tata!"

José and Olive set the content of the trunk onto the backseat of the Citroen DS to make room for the Corsican. He tried to resist, but the Spaniard who had had enough of the thug, hit him in the head with his gun and knocked him unconscious. Olive drove the car leisurely along the Mosel River; they were in no rush to go anywhere since they hadn't decided what to do next with their prisoner.

"Some of the stuff you said about Corsica was pretty extreme; I hope you don't hold half of that sentiment against the island and its people," Schneider probed.

"Nah, I love Corsica and its folks; it's a beautiful place full of noble souls. I wouldn't mind living there, but it's true they're not too fond of leftists in general. On the other hand, I'm kind of tired of politics, so..."

"You made it sound like all Corsicans were inherently corrupt; can you elucidate?"

"Do the Sicilians or the Calabrese love the Cosa Nostra or the 'Ndrangheta? Suffice to say that being Corsican doesn't mean you belong to the drug clans; that would be dangerous profiling. No, I believe the majority of Corsicans are honorable people. I think you're reading too much into my anger towards that murderer. He was gonna take Stefan down—you know that, right?"

"I do. I get it, José; I just wanted to make sure."

"You showed what you were made of back

there—pretty impressive if I may say so."

"It's not like I haven't been there before; I've seen my share of lowlifes."

"So, how are we going to send the package back to where it came from, and what message do we attach to it?" José asked.

"I don't think we can put him back on the train; someone needs to drop him there. I could possibly arrange something with the department. What if we were to arrest him on charges of attempted murder for that guy Jimmy and send him back to Schmitt in handcuffs? It's just a thought."

"The thing is, if they don't kill him down there, he'll be back to finish the job. Which means you, Stefan, and I will top his hit list; not to mention the danger he will pose to Johnny, Suzanne, and the twins."

"Yes, it's a bad idea," Olive agreed.

"What d'you say I turn him over to the Sicilians down in Marseille for having tried to mess with the Amsterdam run? I'm sure they'd think of something to do with him, notwithstanding the news would reach Schmitt as well.

"Brilliant! Are you sure you can you arrange for it safely?"

"Safe is a figure of speech in this business, Olive. But no, I don't have to expose myself; I'm the supervisor, remember? I have people who get paid to do the dirty work."

"If I hadn't been directly involved with this, I'd probably think using the judicial channels would be the way to go, but the law doesn't always work for the good guys, and if we don't get rid of him fast, there will be much trouble ahead. If it has to look like he blotched the job, what better way than having him entangled with the mafia? I think it's perfect," Schneider said.

"So, let's park in the underground garage. I'll call from *the office* to arrange for a transfer in a discreet location."

At twenty-three thirty, a Ford Transit van pulled behind Olive Schneider's DS whose plates had been switched. The rendezvous had been set in a clearing of the twenty-five-thousand acre *Haye Forest*, bordering Nancy. The Corsican was dragged by two burly men and thrown into the back, where he was propped against spools of heavy flax rope. On José's recommendation, Olive had remained behind at *the office*. The Spaniard hugged the men. The two vehicles took off in opposite directions, under a sky devoid of stars.

26 – JULIA'S STORY (Sun)

Olive and José returned to Toul the next day. The group gathered around the kitchen table in order to assess the latest developments. Julia and Stefan were to be taken away from the greater Nancy area, in case Schmitt decided to send in the big dogs. There was also the possibility the Toul safe house was jeopardized and that the couple and their children had to move as well. José, taking advantage of the twins being busy playing in the living room, explained in depth what had happened the day before, as to maximize the importance of the imminent changes. Julia had narrowly saved Stefan's life. The knife that was supposed to slice his throat belonged to a reliable hitman of the Marseille mob.

"'Reliable,' as in stealthy and efficient—we got lucky," José stressed.

It was too much of a close call to be taken with laxity. Suzanne and Johnny would be thinking about their options, while it was clear the teens had to move within the next days. Schneider highlighted the dire importance of *the Couple* being on the hunt as well, namely that Jablonsky would be in town until he no longer needed to. It was assumed the Corsican had called Marseille after he left Jimmy's place to keep Schmitt in the loop; meaning Stefan's name had most likely been associated with the girl. Olive was certain the chief of police had asked to be kept informed, since, as she stated, he was afflicted with the compulsion to orchestrate. So, following that logic, Stefan knew too much and had to be eliminated.

Schneider proposed to take Julia back with them

to *the office*, where she could share all she had for cross-referencing purposes. Names had to be matched to faces, and vice versa. Too many of the elements that needed to see the light converged in a room full of smoke and mirrors. If Olive was to use her leverage in the force, she needed a lever, which pointed towards completing the mapping she had started, and making some of the faces talk. She would have to start with her own department, to establish how it colluded with Schmitt, who was once in charge of it. How Vidal's relationship with the Marseille superintendent had influenced the way Julia Feraez's case files had been manipulated. And or course, nothing could be done in the open. Olive Schneider accepted that, in joining the Spaniard, she had diminished her role in the police in favor of one in the world of undercover agents; except she wasn't CIA or DST, at best, she volunteered as a contractor operating for the FBN, but not even; she was simply a rogue *Police Nationale* officer, a renegade, who by having involved herself in the concealment of the Corsican, had become complicit in the use of illegal procedural methods. She understood that the path chosen couldn't afford to arrive at a cul de sac, for it would become her cell for the rest of her life.

The phone on José's desk rang. The Spaniard picked it up and smiled before hanging up without saying a word.

"One of the associates is arriving in a half hour, her name is Corinne Jones, a dual citizen of France and the U.S. I'm glad she's coming; we could use all the help sent our way. I think you two will work well together."

José said, addressing Olive Schneider, who had put her arm around a visibly distraught Julia.

"Lovely, but our girl is finally catching up with the emotional toll of the last few days. Let's not overwork her," she implored.

"I understand that we could be unearthing old wounds, but Julia, here, can tell us when too much is too much, right?"

"I'll be OK, it's just a pang."

"So, let's get started, will we? Beginning with you oldest memory, what can you say about the men and women that you believe were culpable of abusing orphans?" Olive asked.

"It started with the nuns. I remember one pulling me by the hair and washing my mouth with Ajax scouring powder for talking too much. It was horrible, it burned my eyes and she beat me for screaming; I was terrified. It felt like that one nun jumped at every excuse to be mean to me. Others were just as scary, threatening to send us to Hell for punishment. That was when men would come to fetch groups of children that had "misbehaved." We would never see them again."

"And that was Marseille, right?"

"Yeah."

"If I were to show you photographs of the men who took the children away, would you be able to recognize them?"

"I don't know, maybe."

"Later I will show you the pictures I have, but for now, let's move the clock forward. What happened later?"

"Well, my turn came to be sent to Hell for screaming too much during punishment. I remember the man who took us away; he had a burn mark like José, except his was really pink and the eye on that side of his face was blind and kinda light grey."

"I know who that is; his name is Giuseppe di Giovanni, originally from the Cosa Nostra; he's currently working out of Bastia. He's also made the FBN list," the Spaniard cut in.

"So, what happened next, Julia?" Olive asked.

"We were four, two girls and two boys. He took us to a dark basement lined with cots on one side. There was a potty in the middle of the space, smelling of shit and bleach. Then, he left and locked the door behind him. I don't remember how long we stayed in there, but one of the boys and I were taken to a place whose rooms were draped in red velvet, some were green; it was very strange. I felt sleepy, I could hear children laughing, but the laughs were not happy ones, more like they were supposed to laugh. I saw men and women in suits; they looked well-off. They sized us up and down, touching us like we were merchandise. I must have dozed off, because suddenly, me and the boy were naked and I was holding his penis while he urinated on the stone floor; the piss was splashing my ankles. I saw a man taking pictures with a big box camera, and lights behind white umbrellas. For the longest time, I thought it was a dream, and sometimes I still do. Later, the man with the blind eye took me back to the orphanage, but not the boy. I never saw him again."

"You're saying they took the boy?"

"Yeah, the man lived on the compound."

"Here's a picture of a nun, who I believe belonged there; do you recognize her?"

"Yeah, she spoke with the men who visited."

"Do you remember her name; could she have been Sister Chloe?"

"No, I don't think so."

"What about Odile, or Nicole perhaps?"

"Nope, it doesn't ring a bell; I don't think she was French—Italian maybe."

"What about Daniela?"

"Mother Daniela, yes, that's it."

"You're doing great, but I think it's good enough for today. We mostly wanted to take you away from Toul for a while and show you what we're up to. I hope you understand why we blindfolded you before we brought you here; nobody must know about this place. Now, next time you come here, tomorrow or Tuesday, we will ask you to recollect a lot more; so be ready," José said.

"I'll take you back to Johnny and Suzanne's after we meet Corinne," Olive added.

"Thanks, I know Stef is freaked out, but he's trying to be cool. I don't want to leave him alone though, even if he can handle it. Or maybe it's me who wants him around; I'm kind of a mess," she confessed, trying to summon some humor.

27 – CORINNE JONES (Sun)

Olive returned to *the office* after she dropped Julia off. Corinne Jones was an amicable, bespectacled petite, with shoulder-length auburn hair and a slightly upturned nose. Olive Schneider's five foot eight frame and single-braided blond hair contrasted sharply with the newcomer, yet, there was an odd something about the two that made them look like sisters. Perhaps it was the energy, the relentlessness to see through things, the training, and the contagious confidence that emanated through their shared presence that contributed to that impression.

José had antecedently spoken with Corinne about his recent partnering with Olive; she was up to date with the logistics of the agreement to combine information into one case. Jones was prepared to do what it took to add to the pot. She volunteered to drive to Marseille to follow up on the Corsican's fate, and go after whatever lead they may have for her while she would be there.

"The agency is prepared to take action; headquarters deem there's enough information at our disposal to start compromising some public figures and awaken the French authorities to the undeniable presence of bad weeds in their own backyard," the agent stated.

She looked at Olive before continuing.

"You understand that we, the FBN that is, are not in this for the children, that's you and José's department; but the melding of the two cases is such that we often find ourselves wondering what it is exactly we're after. It's hard not to get emotional when we come across the kind of information that highlights some of the mafia's other 'enterprises,'" Jones explained.

"And it's because of the often frequent overlapping of those enterprises that we consider it necessary, at this point, to merge the results of searches, which until now, were barely aware of each other; and often, as in your case, done by private groups or individuals," José added.

"I know why I'm doing what I'm doing, but how do you see that merging in action, my role in it, and how the information I possess is going to help you catch heroin smugglers?"

"We want the French to take care of what's happening in their country. We don't have enough of a staff to apprehend and drag the bad guys into the U.S. judicial system for trial; we don't even possess the legal means to do so, especially when political interests have been putting sticks in our wheels, which of course highlights system corruptions of our own. So, we need you to harness the power to bring the spotlight on our suspects. For that, we encourage you to find others in the force willing to assist you," Corinne said.

"That might prove to be tricky."

"Not if we help you locate them. For instance, there is one such individual in your department and it may surprise you: Ernest Jablonsky, Jean-Marie Vidal's partner. He knew Julia was in Toul when he spotted her downtown, last Tuesday. He followed her to Johnny's place, so he could easily have gotten her back to the precinct by tipping the gendarmerie. He's actually keeping a tab on Vidal, who we believe is working for Schmitt, a pawn of the clans paid handsomely to not only look the other way, but to also use the brunt of his forces for their protection."

"Yes, it's a bloody surprise; but how do you know that?" a stunned Olive Schneider asked.

"Because Ernest Jablonsky also comes to *the office*, that's why."

"You're saying we're going to be working together?"

"No, that would stack the deck to a tipping point. Let's just say you're aware of each other, meaning you watch each other's backs. You get the comfort of knowing you have a friend who will not interfere with your extracurricular activities. He might in fact nudge bits of information your way when he sees fit; which also means you do the same for him."

"You understand I cannot be accountable to the FBN; my allegiance is to the *Police Nationale*."

"Of course, that's the idea," Jones returned.

28 – DI GIOVANNI (Mon)

Erik Schmitt kicked a chair across his office in anger. Not only had the Corsican failed, but he was in the hands of the Sicilians, who threatened Pinelli that if he didn't keep the Bastian clans out of their routes, he would soon join the hitman in swimming with the fish.

"What the fuck happened?!" he thought aloud.

The phone rang. He almost didn't pick it up. The female voice at the other end was to remind him his package had been sent back due to a lack of adequate postage.

"We ensure all returned merchandise are handled with care, but occasionally, a box falls off the stack and gets crushed. I hope the content wasn't fragile. Sorry if it was!" she added, before hanging up.

"Who's that northern bitch?!" he raged.

Corinne Jones hung the handset back on the payphone. She had driven all night before checking in a hotel near *Boulevard des Dames*, by the old port of Marseille. Later, she would connect with one of the offices of the FBN, but for now, she needed to get the feel of her self-made assignment, ahead of engaging the channels. She, for the longest time, had wanted Schmitt to get his ass handed to him, a man she despised with unrestrained passion for his trademark chauvinism. She had briefly interacted with him while in training, before opting to serve her "other country" instead.

Schmitt picked up the phone and called Vidal, who happened to have taken off for Metz in the early morning. Jablonsky answered in his place.

146

"Have him call me ASAP, it's important!" he spat.

"Lieutenant Schneider, the postmaster rang to say your package has been signed for!" Jablonsky called on the intercom, after the Marseille superintendent hung up.

"Thank you, Major!" Olive replied.

It all of a sudden came to her that things were going to be quite different from now on. The presence of an ally in the force, even if they didn't communicate directly, was almost heartwarming. She no longer had to live alone in the secrecy of a double life, for there was now another like her, only a door away. She wondered if others would eventually follow.

Schmitt called Giuseppe di Giovanni. The two arranged to meet at the aquatic club of Marignane outside the Marseille airport. The waters of the *Berre Lagoon* had turned choppy from the wailing mistral.

"Bad news blew with this fucking north wind; the Corsican's been captured by the Sicilians and is probably dead by now. I have no idea what happened, except a bitch called with the intention of feeding me my balls. Something happened in Nancy that smells of fucking trouble. Sergio called me after he supposedly located his target; next thing I hear, he's back in Marseille for having fucked with the mafia's Amsterdam run. Does it make sense to you?" Schmitt raged.

"Sounds like a setup to me, mate. Someone's ahead of your game, and by the look of it, they have you exactly where they want you."

"Yeah, like between two Hells and a bunch of barking puppets. I need to fix that shit pronto!"

"And you count on me to do that for you, I assume. Why? Because you think I can set up a negotiation table between the Sicilians and the Corsicans?"

"No, I want you to do what Sergio couldn't—make that fucking chick disappear before she talks!"

"So, now you want her dead; I thought Graziano wanted to drill her for what she knew."

"What Graziano wants may not outweigh what Pinelli needs erased. What is she gonna do, send you after me?"

"What makes you think she hasn't yet?"

"Because you know as well as I do that her shit will eventually hit the fan and you'll need protection then; that's the what."

"Maybe, but what makes you so sure you'll still be around to give it then? Because based on what you just told me, some of your shit has already splattered some mighty shiny shoes."

"If you help me fix this mess, I'll be around. Think of it as an investment in future security."

"How deep can you go, because with the CIA getting cold feet, we're gonna need a lot of protection from you guys. Are you willing to pay the price?"

"I always pay my debts. You help me now—you've got my word."

Corinne Jones had followed Schmitt to Marignane. It didn't take her long to figure out why he was meeting with the gangster. In the midst of conflict, new alliances had to be made. Over time, Di Giovanni had steadily distanced himself from the Mother Superior to gravitate towards the Corsican clans. He was valuable to them as an ex-Cosa Nostra member in providing tips on dealing with the Turks, and ways of hitting the U.S. market while avoiding the mafia's hot spots. It also showed Schmitt had become aware the winds were turning. She called *the office* to tell José to expect some heat from the south. She would keep him updated.

The federal agent decided to tag the Sicilian after the meeting. It was unlikely he would suspect someone on his tail, but she nonetheless kept her distance. It was better to lose him than blow her cover.

Sergio the Corsican was facing two stocky men with dark sideburns and a golden earring on their left ear; they reminded him of Gitanos. They went by the names of Luigi and Rocco. He was tied to a chair, looking disheveled from the ride and the lack of sleep. He also had urinated and defecated in his pants, stinking the place to high heavens. He knew his hours were counted.

"So, tough guy, who's paying you to fuck with our route?"

"You know damn well I've got nothing to do with your fucking route!"

"Why're you here then?"

"A Spanish whore with a burnt face screwed up my gig, that's all I know. What does that have to do with your fucking heroin?"

"The Spanish whore is the boss, that's why, smart ass. Do I need to repeat the question?" Luigi asked.

At that moment, Giuseppe di Giovanni entered the basement room, hugging the two Sicilians.

"It stinks in here! Did someone step in dog shit?" he uttered, glancing at the Corsican.

"Yeah, I guess I must have dragged it in here under my shoe, my mistake!" Rocco exclaimed.

"So, how did you end up crossing the Spaniard, Sergio; did you confuse targets?" Di Giovanni asked.

"I'm not saying anything to you!"

"OK, let's just imagine I know who sent you up there and for what purpose, would you mind sharing the things I must have missed, because it's your life that's on the line, and talking is time bought," Giuseppe offered.

"So, who sent me then?"

"Does 'continental swine' ring a bell?"

"Let's say it does, what about the target?"

"Black girl, about eighteen, good looking chick; does that work for you?"

"OK, so you know I wasn't fucking with your merchandise then?"

"You explain that to the Spaniard, because he thinks you were."

"You're going in circles, what the fuck d'you wanna know? Oh shit, whatever..."

"Shit it is, Sergio; I thought your kind knew how to hold it in. You should have yourself checked for anal leakage."

"I've got to live with the stench, so the humiliation's on me. This is a mind fuck; both of us are being played. So, what the hell d'you need?!"

"Locations and all the players for a start. Then we can take it from there."

"Would a shower be asking for too much?"

"Rocco, show him the powder room, I think there are extra clothes upstairs that might fit him."

Corinne Jones had parked a way away from the old stone house where she saw Di Giovanni enter. She was in the outermost suburbs of Marseille amid spread neighborhoods of houses on large, walled estates, betraying the affluence of their owners. The property was known by the FBN as being used by the mafia for various reunions and meetings, a place José had visited on occasion. The presence of Graziano's henchman at the house was perplexing, due to the fact the Sicilian was banned by *the family* for his involvement in helping the "French connection." Something wasn't right, and the possibility the Spaniard was compromised arose. If the Corsican was still alive, Di Giovanni would soon be in possession of information that could either serve Schmitt or make him a target of the mob. One way or the other, Jones saw it as a mind fuck of the first order. She returned to the car and drove to the first payphone to alert José who was staying at *the office* for the length of her investigation. It was also time to involve the third partner, Lance Merckx, aka the Rotterdam liaison.

29 – THIRD PARTNER (Tue)

Lance Merckx was a fit forty-two year old with slightly long, light brown hair and pronounced facial features that gave the appearance of having been chiseled. He and José were roughly the same height, around five ten, though he was somewhat stockier than his associate. He entered the room with a thermos of coffee and a briefcase he plopped noisily on his desk.

"It's nice to be back!" he exclaimed, hanging his coat on the freestanding wooden rack.

"Nice to have you back! I didn't want to say too much on the phone, but we may have a situation down in Marseille. Some mortal enemies are apparently sharing the same bed. Remember Di Giovanni, the guy who used to do the kiddy run for the mafia in cahoots with the nuns running the orphanages, and who's now pledging his allegiance to the Corsican clans by helping them steal away business from the Cosa Nostra; well, he seems to be hanging out with his old buddies as if he never left the family. But since Corinne also caught him with Schmitt, we're having an issue figuring out what's going on. It's my opinion the superintendent has hired Di Giovanni to pick up the pieces after Sergio's failure; yet, what is he doing with my guys?" José explained.

"It sounds like we'd better move in quickly if we don't want to see our work unravel and the mission compromised. We've got to intercept Di Giovanni and neutralize him before he even makes it to this area," Merckx said.

"For sure, but you haven't met Olive Schneider,

Jablonsky's superior at the police station yet—she's new to the team. Problem is, she worked with Schmitt for a decade. If the Corsican spills the beans, it won't take long for the super to suspect his protégé's secretary has been snooping in his affairs. The protégé in question being Jean-Marie Vidal, who now has Schmitt's ex-job in Nancy, and most likely doing some dirty work for him. I'm sure you get the drift."

"All the better reasons to stop Di Giovanni. Does the Corsican know who Schneider is?"

"I don't think so, but if Schmitt were to get suspicious and show him a photo, it'd be over." José said.

"Do we know for sure the Corsican's still alive?"

"Nope, Corinne's on it though."

The Corsican wouldn't have been alive if Giuseppe di Giovanni had entered the room only fifteen minutes later. Instead, he was sitting across the table from his interlocutors, freshly showered and wearing clean clothes.

"So let's recap your story, Sergio: Schmitt hired you to fetch Julia Feraez on behalf of Mother Superior Graziano, whose reasons were to interrogate her before making her disappear with the info that could have compromised some of the powers that be. But you failed. Now, you're saying the Spaniard and some mid-aged, kick-ass blonde nailed you when you were seconds away from offing a boy serenading his girlfriend—girlfriend being the black chick, of course. So, what makes you think the boy wasn't family with the boss? You know damn well coincidences are practically the rule in this business. Couldn't you have checked first who the girl was shacking up with?"

"I didn't get hired to do paperwork. Schmitt asked me to bring him the girl pronto and to clean my tracks."

"Problem is I heard from Schmitt that you left a junkie for dead when he wasn't. Good thing he has friends up there, otherwise your mug would be all over the news. So, you got sloppy, which is surprising considering your résumé."

"'Twas not supposed to happen."

"Well, it did and it's fucking unfortunate. Now, we need to put names to your story's characters. First the boy then the blonde; you got names, Sergio?"

"The kid's Stefan Vogt, a fifteen year old runaway from a shit-hole called Fer. The woman, I have no idea, except she packed a P1, which is unusual for a civilian."

"How d'you know it was a P1 and not a P38, they're the same fucking gun, save for the stamp. Did you see the stamp?"

"It's my job to see shit like that; it was a P1."

"So you're saying she's military, or a cop?"

"I didn't say that; but there's a chance she could be a cop, since military chicks don't do combat in France."

"It still doesn't mean she's one, there're lots of unregistered guns floating around. At any rate, that's not giving us a name; plus the drivers didn't recall a woman at pickup. You're sure you didn't make her up?"

"What would be the point of that?"

"To save your ass by compromising the Spaniard; I believe that's what you're doing. I know your clan is trying to take the Amsterdam route away from us."

"You're fucking kidding me!?"

154

"Rocco and Luigi, you guys make it look like it didn't happen, OK?"

The Corsican tried to protest, but his sentence died in a sickly gurgle.

After she called *the office*, Corinne Jones returned to the mafia's house. She fought fatigue with the caffeine pills she always carried on the job; she couldn't afford to take a nap at such a crucial time. Her patience was rewarded with the exit of Giuseppe di Giovanni, followed by two familiar bulldogs, the golden earring wonder boys, as they were known among the Sicilians: brothers Luigi and Rocco Giordano. It could only have meant one thing: the Corsican was history, since they were the two who had received the parcel—there was a chance Olive Schneider wasn't compromised. Her job was done for the day. She rode down the hill, stopped at a café, ordered an espresso, and called José. She then drove back to her hotel by the old port, took a shower, and went to bed.

BREAK

30 – THE MOVE (Wed and some)

A friend of José's, Alban Desfrères, had stopped by early to pick Julia and Stefan up. They would be staying in Reims for a few days before the place in Paris was ready. Johnny, Suzanne, and the twins were also moving out of Toul to return to Metz where they still had an apartment. They would come back eventually after things settled, so they left the furniture and appliances behind locked doors. After hugs and promises of staying in touch, the occupants of the two cars took off in opposite directions.

Stefan deduced Desfrères must have made the route often, since he was bent on describing the points of interest along the way, tour guide-style. The pair played the game of switching places in the front passenger seat of the Peugeot 404, forcing the driver to stop with annoying regularity. Eventually, he asked them to both stay in the back, to which they laughed, as if they had been waiting for that moment to happen. They made it to the Champagne capital by half-past noon, in time to have lunch at a brasserie in the downtown area.

Their temporary camp was an apartment in a modern project on the outskirt of the city, that offered a spectacular view of the magnificent cathedral rising from the center of town. But the rooms were bare and unheated, with just foam pads and army blankets to keep them warm at night. The only appliances in the kitchen were a two-burner hot plate, a stove top espresso maker, and an empty mini fridge. A pot, a frying pan, and an assortment of mismatched stoneware and silverware completed the setup.

They ate canned food and drank from the tap. In the bathroom, which was barely larger than a closet, the half tub and handheld shower would have been a luxury if the water hadn't been ice-cold due to the gas meter having been turned off. It was a dreadful stay.

If Paris was an improvement over Reims, it also came with its own idiosyncrasies. The studio was part of a set of six, built in the back of the stone courtyard of a magnificent building on *Avenue Foch*, in the sixteenth arrondissement—one of the wealthiest of the city, and within a stone's throw of the *Arc de Triomphe*. But though the main tenants lived in luxury and drove very expensive cars, the renters of the studios were prostitutes, referred to as *putes de luxe*, or luxury whores, by the natives. What made these dames "deluxe" was the fact their clientele was flush with cash, and they were self-employed—in other words, no pimps and a high return on services.

Julia and Stefan's studio was sandwiched between Martine and Sylvie's pads, two unique souls as vibrant as they were eccentric. The dwellings were designed for single inhabitants, with an emphasis on space efficiency that rivaled that of a cubicle in a futuristic overpopulated planet. Only the black, wall-mounted rotary phone reminded the occupants that technology was a step behind the latest in aesthetics, and painfully trailing human imagination.

Of the other three tenants, two were gay, male prostitutes, Rémy and Serge. The studios were the brainchild of the "odd son" of the family that owned the building, Alain, a bourgeois leftist of sort—also gay.

Julia and Stefan made the best of the space. Another drawback was the lack of grocery stores in the area, which forced the teens to use the métro each time the small fridge reminded them of its purpose. Because of the scant allowance provided by the network, the couple quickly took heart at learning the art of cooking. At first, they concocted simple meals: omelets, crèpes, and hamburgers; but soon came elaborate stir-fries on brown rice, pies, and even chocolate cake. In just a few days, every space in the kitchen became taken with dried herbs and bulk items in tin cans or canning jars. They had quickly realized that eating in was the answer to healthy and tasty food at reduced cost. Barely a week had passed before they were baking their own bread.

When Johnny eventually checked on them, he was stunned by how they lived.

"You two aren't your regular teenagers, are you? Most of the other places I visit are pigsties, where the kids often eat out of cans they heat up in pots of boiling water. They can't manage their money either; they waste it on pinball machines and candy bars!"

"Even though my dad's an asshole, he's a great cook, and my mom's a fab baker. When you've lived with that kitchen smell and the taste of real food, nothing compares; plus, we try to make it fun!"

"We either take turns or work together when we try new dishes. Let's face it, we've gotta make the best of the situation; it works for us," Julia explained.

But spring was still a couple of months away and things were pretty bad in Nancy and Marseille. José called daily from *the office* with updated news. For now, he, Corinne, Lance, and Olive were expecting the visit of

159

Schmitt's henchmen and were preparing for the worst. His word of advice: You're safe where you are!"

Besides the cooking, the studying, and the love-making, only sparsely interrupted by the inevitable arguments borne of living in tight quarters, there was plenty of entertainment provided by the colorful neighbors. Martine was particularly candid about her work, reporting with predictable regularity on the progress of relationships with steady clients, the arrival of new faces and what existed below them, and how she confronted penis sizes, especially the methods of avoiding penetration when the gentleman was too well-endowed. At times, she sounded like a psychologist breaking confidentiality. In spite of it, she had utter respect for the men whom she relieved of their lust and passions on mink rugs, in the back of Rolls Royce Phantoms, or more riskily, on the king-size beds they normally shared with the queen of the house. A regular client was a mother lode Martine couldn't afford to deride. As a matter of fact, and in spite of the money, there was, oddly, motherly love at the base of it all, a sense of protectiveness and understanding towards these men, who were either too weak to find their moral compass or too hopelessly playful to own one.

Serge and Rémy were in the habit of renting bicycles and taking the group for rides across Paris during the wee hours to reach distant, open-all-night gay restaurants and coffee shops, insouciantly laughing and shouting as they passed the few pedestrians braving the cold, or cut in front of taxi cabs and early commuters, like pavement pirates on a rampage. It was during one of those sorties that Julia and Stefan were nearly picked up by the police, hadn't Rémy deftly guided them through obscure alleys to lose the patrol car.

The gay prostitutes' stories were just as colorful as those of Martine's—if not more. They were by far kinkier, more outrageous, as well as exposing of the irrefutable dangers of being gay in a barely tolerant society; often requiring cross-dressing for "straight men" who couldn't afford to come out. In spite of their effeminate manners, Stefan saw Serge and Rémy as courageous souls, who understood the risks and clearly acknowledged the worst case scenario could sneak on them from left field. They were ready for it, with concealed small handguns and switchblade knives.

31 – OLD WOUNDS (Thu)

Corinne Jones waited outside the commissariat of the 1st arrondissement of Marseille, hoping to catch and follow Erik Schmitt on his way to taking his lunch at his habitual café-bar on the Canebière. It was also the time for his connections to report on various assignments and receive orders. Because of his central position, he was nicknamed *the hub* by the associates of *the office*, a moniker that earned him the distinction of being the prime suspect in their investigation, for whoever came to him was a directional marker to some form of organized, ill-fated endeavor.

Two days before, on Tuesday, he had met again with Di Giovanni, south of town, affirming that he was seeking to employ Graziano's ex-right-hand man to resume with the search of Julia Feraez. So, it appeared that in spite of having enraged the Sicilians with Sergio's failure, he was once again counting on Corsicans to finish the job, unaware Di Giovanni was actually only pretending to work for them, since, as far as Jones saw it, he was a mole of *Cosa Nostra* embedded in Bastia.

Chief Superintendent Joseph Pinelli joined Schmitt inside the café. It was the first time Jones got a positive on a physical contact between the two. The act wasn't in itself incriminating, since both were police hot shots, but when one of the Giordano boys walked in to stand by them as if to take their orders, the tables turned. The FBN agent's trusted Leica M3 made quick work of recording the event—Pinelli had moved in status from theoretical to prime suspect.

162

Jones took it that the lack of vigilance on their part was indicative the meeting was driven by urgency. There was no longer a doubt the Sicilians had reported on the fate of Sergio the Corsican and that some form of negotiation was in process. Still, Corinne couldn't deny observing that Schmitt and Pinelli were being used by the crime families. From the outside, the chief of police was like a revolving door for the gangs to operate along the legal channels. But it was very much unlike him to be unaware of the pattern; thus, he had to have something else going on. Overall, all parties were guilty of trying to outcon each other, unless of course, Schmitt was in such trouble that he could only move forward to not lose face, which was the version Corinne Jones believed to be true.

After Jean-Marie Vidal returned from Metz on Monday, Major Ernest Jablonsky informed him that Schmitt had called, wanting to talk to him urgently. The news was that a Marseille contact would imminently be touching base with him about Julia Feraez. On Wednesday, Giuseppe di Giovanni called from Lyon to tell him he was on his way. Vidal informed his partner to get prepared for action and be ready to assist with all available information, methods, men, and equipment. That same evening, Jablonsky was at *the office* going over details with José Perez, Lance Merckx, and Olive Schneider. It was inevitable the two police officers should find themselves partnering in the end; together, they had the means to slow Vidal down, and eventually, compromise him.

First, Di Giovanni sought to retrace the Corsican's steps, but on José's recommendation, Jimmy had moved out and taken a leave of absence from the bakery. The mafia man also quickly discovered the Toul house had been vacated; though, he intuited its owner and Jean-Michel Tourbé were the same person, and thus, the Spaniard had to be responsible for getting Julia Feraez out of her cell and away from the hands of Schmitt and Graziano. In other words, the boss was protecting the kid and her information, which meant he had an invested interest in complicating life for the cop and the nun. But as Di Giovanni saw it, there was a problem with that, since *the family* didn't necessarily want some of what Julia knew propagated. And though, most likely, the Spaniard had his reasons, he was, knowingly or not, undermining the loyalties between him and his suppliers, and about to introduce bad blood in his relationship with *Cosa Nostra*. But thanks to Jablonsky, José was now aware of what he was up against.

It didn't take long for Di Giovanni to seek a meeting with José; the two rendezvoused at a bar in a small village, twenty kilometers out of town.

They exchanged hugs before sitting at a table in a dark and musty corner. The hum of the forced-air heating system droned over Johnny Haliday's latest hit coming out of the Wurlitzer, which looked downright out of place in a room built in the fifteen hundreds.

"So, I guess you got wind of the Corsican's mishap," José started.

"Yeah, Rocco and Luigi took care of him. He claimed he was working for Schmitt, and most likely, Joseph Pinelli; any truth to that?"

"I'm sure he was, but a knife to the throat of a kid under my protection wasn't the best way for Schmitt to make an alliance. What was he trying to achieve by fucking with me?"

"I have the feeling he didn't know the kids were connected to you."

"Maybe the Corsican didn't know, but that would be a first for Schmitt, in his position."

"It's below my pay grade to ask questions, but any reason why I shouldn't know why you're protecting the one everyone seems to want for what she might know?"

"I'll be frank with you, Giuseppe; the kid's been with me since I rescued her from rapists, nearly four years ago—she's a daughter to me," José answered.

"I knew her at the orphanage ran by Mother Daniela Graziano, down in Marseille. I used to drive the van that brought kids in an out of the place."

"So, you must know what I'm protecting her from. In most cases, I wouldn't have the time to care, but as I'm saying, she's my kid."

"Which, I gather, puts you in an odd position vis-à-vis the family and the cops working for it, right?"

"Possibly, but while she's under my protection, the family has nothing to worry about. As to the cops, they've been playing their own Russian roulette. As far as I see it, Schmitt and his cronies have been nosing into my affairs for too long not to have their hands in too many pots. Schmitt wants Julia, because Pinelli and Graziano are paying him to get her, and now it seems he's hired you to do their dirty work. But when you look closer at the whole picture, Schmitt is aiding the Corsicans in controlling the Amsterdam route."

"Can you back your claim?"

"For one thing, we're finding their heroin inside our market; it's not like you and I can't tell the difference between provenances. They are building their own route using different cities as hubs, but they couldn't go around Metz, and that's why their smack can be found in Trier and Saarbrücken."

"So you're saying Schmitt is working for the Corsicans, and by extension, the CIA?"

"From my perspective, the Americans are pulling out of that deal. They're aware of who's flooding their market with heroin, and their politicians are applying a lot of pressure on them to stop catering to the clans. Plus, the rhetoric about keeping the communists out of the old port has become redundant—Deferre is seeing to it. No, Schmitt is working for Schmitt, because he's an ambitious son of a bitch who never has enough of proving to himself he can outsmart anyone," José said.

"It's my opinion as well, but the family doesn't listen to opinions. Nonetheless, your suspicions corroborate ours; we can tell the math on returns doesn't add up to the demand. But let me ask you, are the Americans setting up a net around the Corsicans?"

"You're asking me as if I should know these things, but yes, they are; and the minute the CIA goes in full reversal, they will put pressure on the French to start sorting out their dirty laundry."

"I gather you're being pretty frank with me, José, so I'm going to confess to something. As you know, I work inside the clans for the family, providing them with tips while I collect as much about their routes as I possibly can. But, it comes with its dangers, and honestly, I'm tired of the game. And now, I'm here on a job that does nothing but highlight the absurdity of my situation."

"So, what are you saying, Giuseppe, you want out? If so, what d'you want me to do about it?"

"It's a confession, not a request."

"Listen, I've been in this business for a long time, long enough to have been made aware of all the traps. You know damn well that this kind of honesty is never honest. Is that another trick from Schmitt?"

"OK, you're not hearing me. I too have been in this business long enough, especially as a mole, to pinpoint inconsistencies. The blonde with the P1 couldn't possibly be working the route, and I know she's not your wife. Since when do you have officials working for you, José?"

"Since when am I not allowed to use the system, Giuseppe; do you think the route has been working that smoothly without it? Everything can be bought if the price is right—one of the basic modus operandi of the mafia, if memory serves. So it's my turn to ask, why are you saying this to me, knowing damn well the kind of damage I can inflict onto you?"

"Maybe I'm just ready to pay the price, José, that's where I'm at. If I'm wrong about you, I guess I've just sealed my fate."

"Perhaps you have, mate, but as I've said, I've been around long enough to understand innuendos and the finer lacing of mafia psychology. For now, it still looks like a setup, so I'm fairly confident your fate has nothing to worry about. When you come up with something out of the box, I'll decide what to do with you." José stamped.

"So, if my fate is safe, what about, 'I'm ready to tell my story to any official willing to lend an ear?'"

"Why did you wait until now; aren't there people you could have talked to, down south?"

"Because, I don't think I can trust anyone down in Marseille. If Pinelli is corrupt, it's likely everyone working below and above him is as well."

"I'm starting to believe you're crazy, Giuseppe!"

"Listen, I grew up around nuns; I was one of the orphans. Mother Graziano brought me with her from Sicily when she was asked to oversee the convents in Southern France. But comes a point when your personal religion clashes with what you're being asked to do. I served all my life, believing I was doing the work of God, but one day, Jesus spoke to me—that was what made me decide to distance myself from the nuns. He said the work of God was to help the children, and that's what I've been doing ever since. It's also the reason why some important figures have been panicking about what the children that were rescued might remember. It's also why I know about the safe houses. Does it now resonate with you, José?"

"I think you now have my attention."

José remained silent for a moment that was more a balancing act on a tight rope than it had anything to do with time. It was too much too fast, at the crossroad of too many probabilities. It was clear Di Giovanni had come to get Julia and was in no place of authority to doubt him in regard to the route; that was Schmitt and Vidal's work if it ever came to it. Therefore, it was likely the man across the table was serious.

"I'm not concerned about what you might tell about child trafficking, but you know damn well that no activity exists independently from the others. Should you succeed at persuading the authorities, you will bring the route down as well. I don't believe an active mafia man is capable of doing that to his own family, unless there is an internal vendetta involved."

"Or unless the family's idea of a gift was a jar of sulfuric acid thrown at a kid's face to remind him where he came from. They owe me an eye and reconstructive surgery, so fuck the family!"

"I was wondering where that came from, pretty nasty present, I hope it wasn't Christmas."

"Sad to say, it was. They told the doctor I was playing in the basement when a vial of acid fell off the shelf. But he had already heard the story a million times; he didn't give a damn, all he knew was that his Christmas was shot too."

Di Giovanni told José that he would think about a way to keep the route out of his confession. But the Spaniard still thought bluff was a possibility, in spite of his near-certainty the Sicilian was breaking down.

"Julia is out of your reach, I made sure of that. If you try to fuck with me, you won't get the luxury of being sent back in a route return van. So, how are you going to explain your failure to Schmitt?"

"I don't have to bring her back, he wants her dead. I'm sure if I tell him the job's done, he'll be more than happy to relay the information to Pinelli."

"That doesn't explain what Graziano will do when she hears you offed her prize."

"My life's always been an abstraction, but I managed to survive."

"If I were you, I might contemplate the possibility that your next bout with sulfuric acid might include the rest of your body," José said.

"As I told you, I'm ready to pay the price, but not

before I have a chance to incriminate those who hurt the orphans."

"OK, I hear you loud and clear; I'll connect you! But I'm sure you and Vidal are going to be busy looking for Julia for a while; Lille and Dunkirk make a pretty good wild goose chase. Why don't you spent a couple of days enjoying the beer and the fries up there, and we'll touch base on your way back?"

"Dunkirk it is, she and her boyfriend tried to get into Britain, but they met their fate on some rotten pier. Schmitt will like the sound of that—Ciao!"

32 – THE INCORRUPTIBLES (Thu)

José, Olive, Merckx, and Jablonsky met at *the office* that night. The news of Di Giovanni wanting to spill the beans was received with renewed enthusiasm for the case. They all knew that at some point people would start talking. Human conscience was a simple process that needed to purge itself regularly; in the end, either guilt or integrity always pushed the doors wide open.

The question of who would be listening remained. The FBN was underfunded, because of the cost of the Vietnam War and the diversion of its resources towards small Vietnamese smugglers at the detriment of larger operations. As a result, it had no leverage on the French justice. As a matter of fact, few in the *Police Nationale* knew there was such an organization operating on its territory. The fact the FBN only employed three fulltime agents in France, and that its name had recently changed to *Bureau of Narcotics and Dangerous Drugs*, made of invisibility a given.

"Whom can we trust in the force to be reliable?" Olive asked Ernest Jablonsky.

"For impact we need superintendents and higher, but I know Frederic Jung of Metz is a good guy who would be interested in exposing a drug ring in his town as well as the rest of Lorraine. Also, George Stiegler in Mulhouse might be receptive to the idea of forming a consortium to fight corruption in the system. Both are superintendents."

"There's also Marcel Paroie in Dijon, whom I know personally. He's an excellent man, with the distinction of being driven by purpose," Olive added.

"Who's in charge of contacting them?" José asked.

"I'll do it, if Olive is willing to team up with me," Ernest volunteered.

"I have worked with Superintendent Alban Vasquez of Reims; I'll pass it by him," Lance offered.

"Corinne is supposed to call any minute now, maybe she knows somebody in the south who might be interested if we have others involved," José added.

Jones called as she promised. She had someone in mind, the chief superintendent of Toulon, Jean-Marc Poitier, as a possible. She also had caught other Marseille officers on film, courting known Mafiosi. She was preparing for return, having been unable to contact the FBN agent stationed in Marseille. She suspected foul play and for that reason, didn't venture visiting the office, even though she had keys. "Just a nasty hunch," she said.

Erik Schmitt had known for a while that he had been followed by an American. He was probably one of the few who knew what the FBN, and its newer version, the BNDD, stood for. He had tried to get his old friends in the CIA to intervene, but he was reminded that the agency was no longer invested in protecting the old port, and thus was incapable of assistance. Feeling that he had been given carte blanche to act as he saw fit, he contracted the golden earring wonder boys to tag the spy and report on his movements daily. Upon informing Joseph Pinelli of the presence of an interloper, the chief superintendent recommended apprehending the man for questioning "the old fashioned way." It was how James Nichols found himself in the basement of a Bastia house, facing Sergio the Corsican—a week before the latter met his fate—tied to a chair and awaiting the arrival of those with whom he had some explaining to do. So, after all, José was right when he suspected the Corsicans to be snooping in his affairs; except, it wasn't the drugs that concerned them, but the fact he was an agent posing as a smuggler. Nichols, who wasn't made of the toughest of fibers, talked until he had to be shut up. The Corsicans knew all they needed to know about the FBN and their agents in France, and were intent on eliminating them all, starting with José. Unfortunately for Sergio, he was the one who got found first, while luck wasn't siding with those who invested in Di Giovanni to take care of business either.

But brothers Rocco and Luigi Giordano had also observed another body spying on Schmitt, Corinne Jones, who was packing her things at the hotel, ahead of her return drive up the Rhône Valley. On orders from Schmitt, they wired a bomb to her car's ignition, down in the basement floor. Problem was, it was a rental the company had agreed to pickup at the hotel. Her real car had been parked in a pay lot by the Hertz office. A taxi took her there. By the time the explosion shook the building, Corinne Jones was passing Avignon, a hundred kilometers north of the metropolis.

The day following the meeting, Ernest Jablonsky and Olive Schneider were able to connect with the list of superintendents they had deemed suited for the task of forming an anti-corruption team. All showed an interest, including Lance's connection in Reims, and pending

Corinne's man in Toulon, they would be able to arrange a meeting with a high official. George Stiegler recommended Inspector General Jacques Febrault, with whom he had trained, and who he believed could be fully trusted. The Mulhouse superintendent offered to contact him with the intention of selling him on the project. Olive Schneider couldn't help notice how much easier it was for men to arrange things between them, than it would have been for her to set the gears in motion. But she was happy with the process, she knew one day justice and equality across the board would be achieved; for now, the primary target was to bring a bunch of powerful men in the same room so that, other powerful men, and perhaps some women, could be brought to face their crimes.

Stiegler called back to inform *the office* that Febrault was willing to meet in Paris the following Monday. Within an hour, all had accepted. The inspector general called Toulon himself to get Poitier on board, as well as a few other seasoned officers, whom he waged were trustful men ready to serve their country to the highest level of allegiance; among them, a controller general, two superintendents, and two commandants.

José saw the synchronistic convergence as the cumulative effect of years of hard work and preparation, but he knew he had to take a step back and forgo the glory, for it was now the time for a change of the guards. He saw himself and his colleagues as the unsung heroes, but he wouldn't want it the other way, for there was no romanticism in fame, and rarely any mystique.

Yet, the work was only beginning. If Di Giovanni was to indeed testify before an official body—same with Julia upon turning eighteen, and notwithstanding what Olive had unearthed in her research—his services would soon be in high demand, such as creating an official branch of child protection, incorporating his network of safe houses—a dream he had been unsure would ever take root.

Superintendent Frederic Jung, in an élan of unrestrained humor, proposed to borrow the moniker *The Incorruptibles* to name the group. Though it was somewhat premature to conceive of the formation of such a team, it sounded like a title that could stick. Olive and Ernest were for it, but it was to be seen if any of the others, outside Lorraine, would feel the same love for it. Time would only tell, as the seasons of man's doings and un-doings cycled in uneasy steps.

33 – PLANS & COGITATIONS (Fri)

The news of the explosion in Marseille made it to *the office*, together with the discovery of James Nichols' body floating in the Berre Lagoon. Though it was unclear what had happened to the FBN agent, it was less so for the car rented under Jones' nom de guerre, Evelyn Chabron. Besides the latter's presumed death, a number of other victims were still buried under the rubble caused by the collapse of the floor above. The associates felt devastated by the loss of the Marseille connection, but also relieved that by following the directives of erasing her tracks to the letter, Jones' life was spared. As Corinne compounded the elements of her mission into a coherent report, there was hardly a doubt Schmitt and the Giordano boys were at the bottom of the attack. The double homicide hid no secret as to how much the operation had been jeopardized. Whether the Corsicans and the Sicilians worked together or independently, it became irrelevant; the mob had caught up with the FBN, and someone would soon be knocking at the door to finish the job. That Friday, José and his wife Lizzy moved out of their apartment into an open safe house in Fer. The irony didn't escape the Spaniard, since all seemed to have started with Stefan Vogt's appearance on the scene.

José's buzz pager let him know Di Giovanni was trying to get in touch. The Spaniard rang back. The Sicilian had called Schmitt to report on the deaths of Julia Feraez and her boyfriend. The superintendent had replied by saying he couldn't wait to read it in the news. Maybe he was just bluffing, but his tone carried an ominous darkness that betrayed ills brewing down-south. José asked him to stick around Lille for a couple more days, until an official appointment could be set up with someone prepared to take down his testimony.

Giuseppe intuited his return to Marseille wouldn't be received with a warm welcome; perhaps the Corsicans had gotten wind of his true role in the clans, or would it be the Sicilians, rather, that wished him dead for having denied Mother Daniela the object of her twisted desire? Di Giovanni knew why the nun wanted the girl so badly: it wasn't as much for what she knew as it was for what she did before running away. Well, actually, she didn't do it, someone else did, but since she was the last one seen with Sister Henrietta before fleeing, she was the culprit. After banging noises and heavy steps were heard in the convent hall, some of the nuns converged on the sister's still open door to confront the sight of her unconscious, half-naked body, a crucifix jammed up her vagina with blood running out of it. She was still holding the whip she had used to punish Julia, and the girl's undies were lying on the floor by the poking iron that had struck Sister Henrietta to the head.

Superintendent Vidal had also been on the phone with Di Giovanni. The sound of "Mission accomplished!" rang like a late Christmas present in his mind. Arresting a subject under fake reasons was one thing; to terminate two youngsters was another man's work. He was glad there were hired hands with the mettle to do the dirty work. Nonetheless, he was perplexed by how the Sicilian had managed to locate Feraez in Dunkirk; none of his leads had pointed in that direction. Logic had dictated that her best moves were either Strasbourg or Paris, the two places where he had informed his contacts of her potential visit, and briefed them on how to proceed from there. He felt discomforted by the realization his input had been ignored in favor of better information, but whose information was it? He had been under the impression Erik Schmitt had handed him the reigns, yet it was obvious Di Giovanni operated from a different set of instructions. When he confronted the Marseille superintendent about it, he was reminded that team work often required the ability to flex when the winds changed direction. "Logic is a good thing, Jean-Marie," he had said, "but human rationale isn't the axis on which the world turns; so when logic fails in favor of the unexpected, sacrifices have to be made."

Vidal wasn't sure what his tutor had meant, but deep down, the insult had come down like a cleaver. He called Jablonsky to his office.

"Ernest, I believe we're being perceived as provincial oafs by Marseille, why is it that we were not informed the girl had ran off to Dunkirk with the kid that went missing a couple of weeks ago?"

"We have no information of a link between the two; there was no reason for one in the first place."

"Then, how come Schmitt knew of one; did Sergio the Corsican provide him with that information?"

"I can hardly imagine the Corsican going back to Marseille without the girl. So, the way I see it, for him to sit across Schmitt and go over the details of his failure, is even less conceivable. If Sergio provided that information, it means he got dragged back down there and he's probably dead by now."

"So, he met resistance in Nancy, if I get the gist of it?" Vidal probed.

"It appears it might have been the case."

"The only way he could have been expected is through us. Is that even possible?"

"Don't forget Marseille; maybe someone down there didn't want him to find the girl. Schmitt's operation may not be as airtight as he thinks."

"It could also mean ours isn't either." Vidal offered.

"Who at the station d'you think could be aware of what we've been up to?"

"Or, onto something of their own... What about Olive, she's the one that let Feraez go in the first place?"

"You're shitting me Jean-Marie; she might be an officer, but she's a woman for Christ's sake. She has no leverage!"

"You're right, she can't provide information she doesn't possess. It was just a thought—so that leaves you and me."

"Brilliant, that went somewhere!" Jablonsky concluded sarcastically.

Erik Schmitt met with Luigi Giordano at the café on the Canebière. He had let Pinelli know of Giuseppe's progress, but the chief superintendent wasn't ready to celebrate quite yet. The Sicilian had bullshitted him with his Dunkirk story. Sure he had called from there, but no underage in their right mind would hole up in the northernmost corner of France with nowhere to go—kids hated shitty weather. Of course, Vidal was right about

Paris or Strasbourg, but he was now inconsequential; he had been a bust from the get-go. His partner Jablonsky had proven to be much more able, but he was a lowly major with limited range.

"Francis Visconti's getting restless and I'm not ready to lose him quite yet. I want you to take him with you, dig Di Giovanni out of his hole, and find the girl. She's either in Paris or Strasbourg; flip a coin. Rocco will stay in Nancy to take care of the Spaniard and the blonde bitch he's working with. Superintendent Vidal and his second will provide you with what you need: details, protection, whatever... I count on you to get the job done; at this point, I don't care if you act like butchers, as long as they no longer breathe. I understand the nun is asking for the kid alive, but mostly because she wants to witness how she dies; so we don't give a fuck about Graziano; she's an old cunt who's going to the same Hell she sent her kids to. All that matters is that Julia Feraez, the little shit she's been fucking, and Di Giovanni are silenced. After that, we can all sleep like babies. There's cash in the usual place, and more when you guys return. You got it? Alright, good luck!" Schmitt said as he stood up, while finishing his espresso.

34 – BNFAC (Mon)

Eleven men and one woman entered Inspector General Jacques Febrault's office at precisely nine thirty on a grey Monday morning that felt like time had slowed and the usual tumult of the capital had been softened by its veil.

The man had arranged for the precise amount of leather chairs to form a semicircle around his desk. There was an air of careful preparation to the setup that betrayed Febrault had worked on it over the weekend. Many of the men rejoiced at meeting again, some who hadn't seen each other in decades. Olive Schneider had come on insistence from Frederic Jung, whom she knew quite well from shared operations between the two neighboring cities. He was the one who called Vidal, requesting her presence in Metz for the planning of another event. Like most of the others in attendance, they had reached Paris the day before; the exceptions were Superintendent Alban Vasquez, who had left from Reims early in the morning, as well as the controller general and two of the commandants who lived in the city.

The first half of the meeting, which focused on the need for an agency capable of addressing the issue of mob-influenced corruption in the force, lasted until noon; the second half was scheduled at fourteen hours. Rather than splitting into groups, as it was generally the norm, all agreed to stick together and have lunch at the same brasserie, a lively and noisy place under a large, arched, iron-framed, glass roof.

Hearty food and wine had turned the second meeting into a much more relaxed affair, which saw work achieved with rare efficiency. The team was made official and active under a special emergency clause, pending its final approval and statutory governmental seal. Febrault would act as the provisional central authority, which stipulated that until further notice, *The Incorruptibles* were now a certified branch of the *Police Nationale*, with incontestable powers over regional districts and their superintendents—its registered name: BNFAC, for *Bureau National des Forces Anti Corruption*. The inspector general promised ID badges would be ready and mailed within days; the photography room was made immediately available. Febrault's office would serve as temporary headquarters, as well as the place for all subsequent general meetings, until regional branches were created. The clerks and other officials, who had joined for the final formalities, were now seen leaving the room. The original twelve shook hands, laughing that they soon wouldn't be able to stand the sight of each other. The day had been a resounding success for the fight against crime and corruption.

Jablonsky had opted out of the meeting for fear Vidal would smell a fish; thus, he became the thirteenth member of BNFAC, Schneider as his proxy. He and Olive were promoted to the rank of commandant, while the others retained their existing statuses. It was meant for the founders of the BNFAC to represent the organization's highest authority, with commandants as its most junior officers. For the time being, the agency would operate in stealth mode, until key corrupt members of the force were apprehended and brought to justice.

The Incorruptibles had a week to catalog their targets ahead of the first strike, scheduled for the following Monday. They would split into two units of six agents; Febrault would remain behind to coordinate moves and police backup. Each team would be deployed to arrest the first group of suspects. Schneider, Jablonsky, Jung, Vasquez, Stiegler, and Paroie were assigned Jean-Marie Vidal; while the others were due to descend on Marseille for the arrest of Erik Schmitt and Joseph Pinelli. In addition, each of the districts operated by the superintendents belonging to the BNFAC would be made immediately available to apprehend members of the drug smuggling routes and their mafia suppliers. The rest would come with time, as its specifics played on a range of parameters more guessed than foreseen.

With the nucleus of the BNFAC formed, Jacques Febrault busied himself with putting together the plans for a larger and far more reaching gestalt. He had waited for the opportunity for such an organization to rise out of its fermenting stage since the end of the second war, and there it was, in his own hands, at his command. He needed foot soldiers, and perhaps they already existed in the form of the *Police Nationale*. But coercing the force into something different, yet the same, posed an issue of mixed agendas that was difficult to reconcile. BNFAC had to become an overseer, an authority that could harness existing groups, such as the police and the gendarmerie. But it was already the role of the Ministry of the Interior, which in his views needed a stronger spine. Perhaps there was still room for a new branch, like

Development had with the planned Ministry of Territorial Cohesion. He realized the thought was ostentatious, but it had appeal as long as hubris was kept under control. Febrault was ambitious, but he knew where the line was and how to not cross it. He had seen too many of the men he once called his friends, fall for the lure of power, and soon, some of them would join the ranks of criminals under the axe of the new agency. He had witnessed the corrupt seize power during the war, the creation of the Vichy government led by men once recognized as heroes, but soon to become the fallouts of moral bankruptcy and the subjects of disgrace. The BNFAC would stand as a proud organization, regardless of where it belonged and the powers it summoned. They were and would remain *The Incorruptibles* until their purpose reached its end.

35 – THE WONDER BOYS (Tue)

Superintendent Jean-Marie Vidal met with Rocco Giordano at the *Jean L'Amour* brasserie on Stanislaus Square. In spite of Schmitt's insistence on having Jablonsky work with him, he had sent the major across the Meurthe River to take down a deposition from the victim of a robbery. It wasn't suspicion, but rather, pride that was behind the choice. Vidal had been feeling belittled by his tutor's superiority of character, and thus yenned to prove himself to him. Nonetheless, Jablonsky was able to make eye contact with the mobster from a distance before being sent on his way.

But nothing prevented Lance Merckx to inconspicuously sit a few tables away and get a visual on the meeting. Corinne Jones was also in the area with her trusty Leica to record the encounter. It was all that was needed to convince the FBN that Schmitt's hitmen were in town, and the BNFAC that Vidal was knee-deep in the irreversible process of incrimination.

As expected, Rocco Giordano learned nothing he hadn't already heard from Schmitt, but Vidal was willing to provide protection and take care of the cleanup.

"Erik wanted your partner around for this; why did you send him away?"

"We're still trying to act like cops, so he's on business. I'll make sure to brief him. There's nothing he knows that doesn't go through me first," Vidal replied.

"You're sure about that; yous guys piss and shit together? I mean, don't you keep eyes outside when you've got your pants down? I'm sure he sees things you can't possibly see while you're shaking your dick in the *pissoire*," the golden earring wonder boy candidly asked.

"Pretty florid, but you're right, he has my back when I'm on the shitter," Vidal returned sarcastically.

"As the boss says, two sets of eyes are better than one. What about if he knows where the Spaniard and his wife are holed up; or that blonde chick that handed the Corsican his ass to him; or the fucking bastard we haven't offed yet from the Yankee narcs outfit...? Is that stuff he knows that went through you first?"

"Why, that's a fucking logical fallacy; of course he couldn't possibly know that if I didn't already!"

"Alright, just checking, but next time, make sure he's available," the Sicilian said sternly.

Rocco Giordano's looks and style instilled a visceral dislike for his character deep inside Vidal's innards. He was the kind of individual he was in the habit of incarcerating rather than serving. He represented yet another stabbing wound courtesy Erik Schmitt, his tutor, but this time around, it registered as a strong seismic tremor across the strata of his being. For once, he accepted the notion that Schmitt was nothing short of a rude, manipulative asshole that had humiliated him one time too many. In a rare moment of lucidity, he saw a picture of himself spiraling downwards, but that disappeared in a flash when Rocco Giordano required his attention.

"You're with me, man?" he asked.

"Just thinking; you're sure your Spaniard lives in Nancy, not just passing through?"

186

"I got it out of a man who died from knowing it; that's as certified as it gets. Most likely he knows you and your partner, prolly why he was expecting the Corsican."

"You're saying he got the info when I did?" an incredulous Vidal probed.

"Ever wondered why everything you do fucks up; I mean, has it ever occurred to you that your department could have eyes on your movements?"

"You have an eye fetish, but yes, I have and so far, I have no reason to believe there's anyone in my department I should worry about."

"A blonde with a P1 doesn't ring a bell to you?"

"I'm not in the habit of dealing with James Bond characters, but I'm sure if one had come my way, I would have noticed."

"It's possible the Corsican made that one up, but one can never assume. Let me know if something suddenly juts out of your memory."

"So, let's say the Spaniard is here, how do I recognize him?" Vidal asked.

"You were slow coming to it, man; what about burn marks on his face—a gift from Franco?"

"You must be kidding, you mean Perez?!"

"You know him as Perez, I know him as the Spaniard; we have a match, man, brilliant! So now, can we narrow it down?"

"The guy we know is a rabid revolutionary who's notorious for visiting the tank with extraordinary regularity. I very much doubt he would be the type to operate in the shadow. If anything, he's the antithesis of it—a real nut job of a guy—a local hero for the desperate. We probably have his picture on file."

"No bother, anyone else?"

"No, too many Spaniards in this area to assume there's only one with burn marks. You've got to admire the Corsican for finding him so fast in this haystack."

"More like he was drawn to a trap; that's a different kind of skill. At any rate, I know how the Spaniard looks like, cuz us two go way back; me and my bro set him up with the merchandise. So, if I stick around this shit hole long enough, we're bound to run into each other."

"And you don't know his name?"

"You gave me Perez, one of the most common surnames in the Spanish-speaking world; what are the odds he's Perez too?" Rocco teased.

"You've got a gift for sarcasm; I'll give you that."

"It gets better as you kill more people."

Luigi Giordano was not in the habit of complicating his life, so he did just as Schmitt had said; he flipped a coin and got Paris. But first he had to locate Giuseppe Di Giovanni who was still either in Dunkirk or slowly nudging his way back to the only place he could possibly want to live and die—the south. Based on his calculations, south of Dunkirk could still be north of the line that joined Paris to Strasbourg, which Nancy bisected. And since he was presently across Stanislaus Square keeping an eye on his brother, his search area was well defined. But while he had Rocco and Vidal's backs, Corinne Jones was having a field day taking his picture in various poses of vanity, including grabbing his genitals at intervals, as if to make sure they were still where they belonged—a tic that both amused and disgusted the agent.

Luigi didn't see anything out of the ordinary, except for a second, he thought some guy a few tables over was being curious; but it was just a false positive. Visconti was meant to report from Toul imminently. Rocco had sent him—just in case—on a reconnaissance of the house where the Corsican had found the girl and her boyfriend, and where he was busted by the Spaniard and his sidekick. Just like clockwork, he returned in time for Jones to record the reunion on her M3.

Since the man Ernest Jablonsky had met with was in a hurry to go elsewhere, the major, instead of getting back to the station, thought it to be a good idea to stop by the square to check on things. He pretended he had business to conduct at the main post office, to position himself at one of the corners of the square in order to locate the key players. He was surprised to find Francis Visconti, the CPS agent who had come for Julia Feraez that Monday morning a couple of weeks back, in the company of whom he recognized from photos taken by Jones in Marseille, as being the brother of the man having a chat with Vidal across the plaza. It was exactly what Jablonsky needed to establish a certified link between Social Services and the mob. It was a good thing Vidal had sent him away, for he now had a vantage view of the situation. The superintendent was to miss on the irony.

Later that night at *the office*, notes were compared. It was deduced Rocco Giordano was in charge of locating José, and possibly, Olive Schneider; while his brother, Luigi, and the CPS agent, Francis Visconti, would be going after Julia, Stefan, and Giuseppe di Giovanni. It was obvious Schmitt hadn't bought the latter's story of having completed the job in Dunkirk.

The time would have been ideal for the arrest of the mobsters while they were still together, but on what counts? Vidal was protecting them, and until they were caught red-handed, nothing would stick.

All the members of the NBFAC were updated on the latest developments, promising their forces would be available for action starting Monday. Jacques Febrault was in charge of covering Paris, Alban Vasquez would be controlling the area south of Lille, while Frederic Jung would oversee Lorraine, including Vidal's jurisdiction. In case things moved south of the Paris-Strasbourg line, Marcel Paroie, George Stiegler, as well as the superintendents picked by Febrault: Claude Henry, from Limoges, and Jules Broussard, from Orleans, would be on the lookout. Alongside dealing with the mob, the planned operation for the arrests of Vidal, Schmitt, and Pinelli was being fine-tuned; at which point, Ernest Jablonsky and Olive Schneider would supervise the district of Nancy. Monday was the day it would all start, a date of future commemoration for *The Incorruptibles*, and in the shadow of the ceremony, for the associates of *the office*.

36 – BEN HAYES (Wed)

Ben Hayes lived in Oakland, California. He was studying nuclear engineering at UC Berkeley, with the intention of working on one of the U.S. submarines patrolling the seas. His father, a decorated, retired rear admiral whose fleet chased and sunk German ships during Second World War, was stationed in Marseille from the end of the conflict to 1956, before being put in shared command of the San Francisco naval shipyard at Hunter's Point, one of the three main stations on the bay, with Treasure and Mare Islands.

Alexander Hayes and his wife, Aurora, were unable to have children, and so adopted Ben from a Marseille orphanage the year before moving back to the States. The navy man had suffered a humiliating injury caused by shrapnel from an enemy shell, though his dignity was left intact. The Hayeses were also black.

Though Ben's real name was Amadi Feraez, his adoptive parents had re-christened him Benjamin, for it was a time of deep pride in all things American, and Amadi wasn't resonating with that spirit.

Ben knew he was adopted at age five, but showed no desire to reconnect with his roots. He had been told there was a younger sister, whom he was separated from the day his biological parents were murdered in the south of France, but it didn't feel the memory was his—more like external information handed down to him rather. He actually had no recollection of his time living in Marseille, or of meeting his foster parents and how they ended up moving to the States. There was nothing there.

Alexander Hayes had recently returned from a reunion of Second World War combatants in France, which he had organized conjunctly with other black officers of the various branches of the military. That was how he had met Bernard Carlson, a retired U.S. Air Force captain married to a French woman and residing in the eastern province of Lorraine. Since he and Bernie adopted children from the same area at around the same time, it was all that was needed for them to become fast friends.

During a lengthy walk along the Seine, one evening of the week-long reunion, they shared stories of life after the war, the choices that were made—the good and the bad. They talked about the compromises black officers had to make after having fought side by side with their white counterparts, feeling a distant sadness, a longing for better recognition. But they considered themselves privileged to have had the education that lifted them up to the higher rungs of the social ladder; for that they were thankful. They also talked about their children, of the difficulties that came with trying to create bonds that weren't there to begin with; and later, having to explain to them that they once had biological parents, at the risk of loosening those fragile ties. It was how Bernie came to hear the name of Amadi Feraez and quickly forget about it. At parting time, the friends exchanged addresses, with promises to keep in touch.

Bernie has been back for nearly two weeks when the subject of the new friend from California came into conversation with his wife Olive. The cause of the delay wasn't due to emotional distance in their relationship, rather, Olive's work at the department and Bernie's research for a book he was writing about his war exploits were at fault. The little time they had together generally happened when they crossed paths in the kitchen, while fixing themselves something out of the fridge, or during the occasional meal at a neighborhood eatery. Recently, Olive had stayed up late working, affording Bernie to bury himself in his papers. So, on that particular Wednesday evening, while police lieutenant Schneider, also commandant in the BNFAC, waited for elements to coalesce, she took Bernie out to a fancy downtown restaurant for some quality time.

"The Hayes couple were stationed in Marseille after the war and adopted a kid before returning to the U.S.," Bernie explained.

"When was that they adopted?"

"Within a year of us, isn't that uncanny?"

"Indeed, and out of Marseille, you're saying?"

"That's right, no wonder we hit it off," Bernie said, laughing.

"So, you had a men's talk about it; do you care sharing what came out of it?"

"Same stuff you and I always philosophized about: the joys and angsts of seeing them grow and find their own paths. In their case, their son, Ben, chose to follow in Alex's steps by joining the navy."

"I guess they must have renamed him, unless he came without a name; Ben isn't exactly French, is it?" Olive wondered.

"No, he actually told me, but I forgot. It sounded like a mix of African and Portuguese—the kid's black."

"It would make sense, particularly in the States, to change your children's first names."

"What makes you say that; we have many foreign names in the U.S.?" Bernie countered.

"I've always had the impression that it was best to fit in than be different, especially in those days."

"Well, there is truth to that, but I prefer to not dig too deep. Anyway, Amani, or Amadi was their son's original name, if I recall."

"Did your friend and his wife ever try to locate the biological parents?"

"No, they had died on the streets of Marseille—part of the collateral damage of a war between two mob families—a bomb, I believe."

"It kind of rings a bell; I've got to check with some people. You're sure you can't remember the family's name?"

"As I said, baby, it sounded Portuguese."

"Thanks, so you had a great time, I gather; any old acquaintances looking to start new trouble?"

"You know, they already have all the trouble they need with the Vietnam War over there; I believe they're ready for more happy news in their daily papers. Plus, that Nixon guy is a real loose cannon."

"How could they elect such a liar; the man is appalling!"

"We, Americans, are an odd bunch!"

37 – TENSION BUILD-UP (Thu)

Olive Schneider called José Perez at *the office* early Thursday morning. She had woken up with the nagging feeling there was something odd in the conversation she had with her husband the night before. The Spaniard wasn't around, which frustrated her. Julia's file was also gone from the cabinet, indicating someone had removed it with the intention of making it like it never was there; probably the work of Vidal. She was tired of the game, of having to pretend everything was OK when obviously it wasn't. She was feeling extremely restless, fearing that the more time was spent in inactivity, the better the chances for the bad guys to slip between the fingers of the BNFAC. Vidal was keeping her busy with mundane tasks, which did nothing but slow time even more. The superintendent had used the station as his private plaything, corrupting the very fiber of its intended purpose by redistributing its functions across areas that benefited his special agenda. She was disgusted by the hubris behind such a deceitful deed, the silent manipulation that had steadily made its way into the everyday responsibilities of his team towards serving and protecting the public. He had betrayed his profession in the most abject of fashions, by endangering the very souls he had sworn to keep out of harm's way. Olive opted to take the rest of the week off on pretext of feeling a cold coming; she turned to her boss, who was sitting at his desk, across the open partition.

"OK with you if I swing by the doctor's office and get myself a prescription for a few days off; I'm not feeling so well?" she said.

"Can't you just take a tablet?" Vidal returned.

"Why, do you actually need me to go over the same files in perpetuum? I can't say we're swimming in new cases, plus Sterns can take over."

"Not everything is in the open right now; I need everyone at their posts to get prepared for action."

"So, you want me behind the typewriter, ready to strike; am I getting this right?" she asked sarcastically.

"It's just that you took off a couple of Tuesdays back; then Jung wanted you in Metz last Monday. I also called your house the day before and a few other times in the early evening since then; d'you know what Bernie said? He said you were busy working on cases! I gather he obviously wasn't talking about police cases. For now, I need you around, so that I don't have to get suspicious," the superintendent said.

"I'm going to the doctor anyway; what are you gonna to do, arrest me?"

"If he sends you home, I'll make sure to have Muller check on you. I can't afford to have you take off whenever you wish, so that you can work on those cases Bernie was telling me about."

"Bernie has no idea what I work on. If I'm busy, it's a case to him."

"At any rate, make sure to get a written statement from the doc for our records."

"I'll leave at noon, so that Muller gets a chance to prepare for surveillance," she returned acidly.

Jablonsky entered Vidal's office, looking incensed. He dragged a chair to his partner's desk and sat loudly.

"What's the scoop with the mess in Toul? I know Visconti was there yesterday, so don't tell me the news hasn't caught up with you," he fumed.

"Calm down, Ernest, we're following Erik's directive; no more Mr. Nice Guy," Vidal returned.

"How can you say that? He gored the neighbors, for Christ's sake!"

"He did? I thought they were robbed."

"I guess that's what the papers and the radio are going to be blaring, and I suppose we and the gendarmerie will be looking for whoever did it?"

"That's the idea, mate."

"Did he have to kill them though, I mean, even if they talked, weren't we covering his ass?"

"I agree, but we've committed to it. Call it collateral damage."

"Where's Visconti now?"

"He's got his lead. Tourbé, or whatever his name is, took off our way, or possibly Metz; and the kids headed west. He left for Paris early this morning."

"And the Giordanos?"

"Luigi's working on Di Giovanni, heading north, and Rocco is looking for the Spaniard and his friends in town, just as it was planned."

"You're aware by now that it's looking more and more like a mob job than a police one. You're OK with that?"

"If superintendent Schmitt says it's a critical case, then it's got to be. It's my job to comply if he asks for assistance, any issue with that?"

"It's my job to make sure the line hasn't been crossed, and with Visconti's carnage, I'm fairly sure it has. I'm surprised you're taking it so laxly."

"If the line is crossed, it's for Erik to answer. I'm sure he can provide an end to his means; he didn't get where he is without having proven what he's made of."

"I hope you're right, I wouldn't want to have to explain this in front of a judge," Jablonsky said, probing.

"What judge, it's not like the law is above us?"

"I guess you're right, we're the law."

"Glad you finally got it! By the way, I was going to ask Muller, but he's busy; can you please keep and eye on Schneider, I think she's up to no good."

"What now?"

"She's off for a few days because of the flu. Let me know if she's leaving her house, that's all."

After Jablonsky departed the office, Vidal called Chief Brigadier Muller in.

"George, I need you to watch the major's back; that's your job for the rest of the week. Report daily, and directly to me, got that?"

Ernest Jablonsky made eye contact with Olive Schneider on his way out. She understood by his signal that the coast wasn't clear to meet at *the office*. It also meant he would be waiting for her outside for a brief update. When she got out at exactly twelve, he was in the hall, pretending to be busy with a notice on the bulletin board.

"I heard you weren't feeling well; I hope it's nothing. Stay warm!"

He shook her gloved hand, slipping her a note she immediately put in her pocket. She thanked him and left the building. He resumed with his reading.

Olive caught a bus to the doctor's office. She waited to be seated before unfolding the note.

"Vidal has put me in charge of recording your movements – he smells a rat. I think he has Muller watching me as well, but he's going to be on break from 13:00 to 15:00, so meet me at the office after your appointment; José should be there by then."

Schneider felt a pang. She ripped up the note and dumped the pieces in a waste bin on her way out. Everything was coming to a tension. Vidal was showing instincts that reflected his training with Schmitt. She was afraid he was steadily catching up with her, and by the look of it, Jablonsky as well.

The doctor was a friend who was willing to help around stressful police matters. She prescribed rest and tisanes for her ailments. Olive had the rest of the week off, finally relieved to not have to be around Vidal until his planned arrest on Monday. She hopped on another bus to get to within a quarter mile of *the office* and walked the rest of the distance, avoiding the avenue. When she made it there, all the associates were waiting for her.

"It appears we have a situation," Corinne said.

"Yes, we're all jeopardized—well, except you who're supposed to be dead," Olive replied candidly.

"Even though we have enough on Visconti and the Giordanos to book them, we've got to wait until Monday to strike. I understand it's frustrating to sit on so much and feel so powerless. But the minute we arrest our three main suspects, the entire *Police National* will be on the hunt for those thugs. Hopefully, their targets will outsmart them until then," Jablonsky said.

"I'm not worried about us, but the kids, Johnny, and Suzanne are at risk as long as those guys are still roaming," José said.

"True, but are you sure you and your wife are safe in Fer?" Olive asked the Spaniard.

"The steel mill and its five thousand workers are a blessing – lots of Latinos and Arabs to get lost in."

"If you say so. But on a different topic, I've got something for you, José. My husband met a new friend from California who adopted a son from Marseille around 1955. Though the kid's name is Benjamin Hayes, Bernie claims his original name was Amani or Amadi, followed by a Portuguese or Spanish-sounding surname. Could he be Julia's brother?"

"Yes, Amadi Feraez's the name; that's uncanny."

"That was my guess, but I didn't want to celebrate too early. I think we could look into it to make sure; that'd save her the trip to Marseille."

"Wow, some good news for a change!" Lance Merckx exclaimed.

"Talking of news, do you know what Visconti did in Toul?" Jablonsky cut in.

"I'm afraid to guess," Corinne Jones said.

"Yeah, he butchered Johnny's neighbors after he got the info he needed. Now he's on his way to Paris to look for Julia and Stefan. The worst part is that Vidal thinks it's standard procedure. I'm not sure whether he's a total puppet of Schmitt's or just as bad as him."

"Either way, he's corrupt beyond repair and his ass belongs in jail. At any rate, I'll be working here until Monday, pending it's safe, since Vidal has me under surveillance from Ernest, who's himself under surveillance from another Vidal pawn, George Muller," Olive said.

"I've also got Muller under watch by one of my men, which makes for a situation bordering on the absurd. So, while you stay here, Olive—since you're technically off and at home—I'll be on duty on Hill Street, sitting in my car across your house, making sure to inform Vidal whenever you leave your place. I too can't wait for Monday!" Jablonsky sighed.

38 – THUGS ON THE MOVE (Fri)

It didn't take long for Rocco Giordano to realize the Spaniard was a step ahead of him. But somehow, that was the way he liked it. It meant the boss was still the boss, even if he was the target. There was pride in knowing that all these years, he had dealt with a man with balls, enemy or not. It made for an even fight, a noble fight whose apex was the glory of death. He felt good. He would deal with the blonde bitch and the U.S. agent later – one thing at a time. Maybe he'll even get lucky and stumble onto the three of them together, though he was unclear on how he would have the upper hand. He was quick to realize Vidal was a pawn of Schmitt's, a pompous ass, who thought he could use his department as he wished. The golden earring wonder boy could see when a man's luck was about to run out, especially a soft man like the superintendent who didn't have the grit to pull himself up when the slope got slippery. He spat on the ground as if to echo his thoughts.

Rocco Giordano imagined what he would do if he were the Spaniard, aware someone was closing in for the kill. He would want to mix in with the crowd, no doubt. France was full of Italian, Portuguese, and Spanish immigrants, who had fled their impoverished countries to help rebuild one that was fortunate enough to still hang to a powerful past. It was a matter of finding where these workers were concentrated in order to get moving. As it turned out, Fer was number one on the list of candidates. The Sicilian drove his red Alfa Romeo 105 Giulia Sprint GT Veloce the ten kilometers of Route 54 to the mill town. He parked by a Co-op market, where Algerian male shoppers waited in line for their turn to be served. He asked around if anyone had seen a man with burn marks on his face—a friend of his. One pointed in the direction of a hill crossed with rows of blue collar housing, newer as they got higher and farther away, until they abruptly stopped at the edge of the forest. When he got to Robert Schuman Street, the last before the trees, he stopped again to ask the same question, but to no avail. He drove to the center of town, parked the Alfa, and entered a bar teeming with regulars. By midday and a few drinking facilities deeper, he had confirmation the Spaniard was holed up somewhere in Fer. It wasn't easy being a new face with easily recognizable features in a small town, even if it was full of Mediterranean types. People simply couldn't stop talking when asked the right way, so hiding was futile; which had Rocco wonder why the Spaniard chose such a place. It could have been a trap.

But now that he knew where his target was, he would take his time, relax some; get psychologically prepared to face a serious adversary, an old friend, who according to the Corsican and Schmitt, was a tool of the Americans. All these years of doing such an impeccable job; it almost didn't make sense. But Rocco knew Sergio had not lied to him; that went for the blonde with the P1 as well—she existed and would be found. He returned to Nancy. He felt like fucking some more with Vidal.

Luigi Giordano had no idea how he would get to Giuseppe Di Giovanni. He drove his matching yellow 105 Giulia Sprint GT Veloce to Reims, from where he would

203

decide what to do next. Just like his brother, he relied heavily on instincts, having learned early in life that blind faith yielded better results than the intellectual deductive process alone. It was inconceivable Di Giovanni would be hiding in one of the northern cities; Reims was more his style, a place where emperors and kings were crowned, a town that smelled of history, of must and old decaying stone. But Luigi's yellow Alfa would be nothing short of a wasp buzzing around Superintendent Vasquez's garden. The Reims cops were ready in case he would show up their way.

But if the wonder boy knew he was expected, he didn't seem concerned. Actually, the police was the least of his worries; they were inefficient and easily fooled. They had been a plaything since youth, the targets of pranks and ridicule. He was free; no-one and nothing ruled over him, not even the fear of getting caught or killed one day—otherwise, he and his brother would have chosen another line of business.

Francis Visconti had no idea either on how to locate Julia and Stefan, but one thing was sure, Jacques Febrault had his number. The double homicide in Toul had made the rounds of the BNFAC, and unbeknownst to him, the CPS agent was a highly wanted man by the Paris police. Unlike the Giordano brothers who adored their Italian cars, Visconti favored train rides and the inconspicuousness of large stations. *Gare de l'Est* and its neighbor, *Gare du Nord*, were to his liking, hubs that buzzed of generic purposes, infinite variations on the one single theme of leaving and arriving. The act of being lost in a crowd with focused commonality made for an ideal cover, a psychological overlay that rendered the observer blind to the obvious. He noticed the heightened presence of armed forces upon his arrival. He was familiar with the scenario from his frequent use of *Gare St. Charles*, in Marseille. It was likely the main gates out of the station were monitored, so he chose the hustle and bustle of the freighting area as his means of exit. He soon found himself on *Boulevard de Strasbourg*, going nowhere in particular. He had no reason to believe the cops were for him, but he needed to clear his mind nonetheless. He called Vidal from a public phone to enquire if Rocco had gotten anywhere with the Spaniard, he needed a lead on the kids' whereabouts. The superintendent asked him to call again later. He had the day to orient himself—to get a feel for the metropolis. Even if he already had visited on numerous occasions, Paris was a chameleon, an elusive host that loved tweaking the nature of the determinable things that strived to become manifest. To the mind oblivious to nuance, it translated as never knowing what to expect with each new visit. You had to live there to experience a sense of reliable fluidity, hence the need for reorientation.

On his ride, Visconti had studied the photos of the teens provided by Vidal; he dumped them in a waste basket upon leaving the car. He knew their age, heights, and was assured there was a great chance they would hang out together. Now, it was a matter of finding them amid the eight and a half million people who lived there. Unlike the Giordano brothers who relied on gut feeling, Visconti believed in precise methodology, given the proper time and space. He hated having to rush, which explained the mess in Toul. Under normal conditions, he

205

would have been able to extract the information without the use of force, but since he was guaranteed protection, what the heck! He thought about the possibilities. Hiding the kids in projects was the most logical choice, but those were generally in the suburbs, devoid of metro access. So, Visconti crossed out the areas outside the city limits, which still left two point three millions residents to sort through. He decided to put himself in the shoes of someone like the Spaniard, a man who had conned the Sicilian mafia for a decade, and with the uncanny ability to anticipate everyone's moves. The safest places in Paris, the ones least likely to arouse curiosity due to their residents' lack of interest in others, were the wealthy neighborhoods. And since well-off African families, as well as black popular artists owned property there, Julia Feraez wouldn't be noticed. Still, it was a single shot in a very dark place, a costly diversion if he were wrong. He would wait for Vidal's info before taking action.

José Perez had gotten the news from Ernest Jablonsky, who got it from Vidal, that Rocco Giordano was sniffing for tracks in Fer. He had somewhat expected the Sicilian would look in the likely places, and thus had asked his wife to go visit her family in Bordeaux until things settled. He wondered how the brothers didn't realize their cars stuck out like sunflowers and bright poppies in a town full of wilted blooms. There were, at best, another couple of red and yellow Alfas inside a twenty kilometer radius. But subtlety wasn't the Giordanos' motto. The Spaniard would simply wait out the time ahead of Rocco's grand entrance.

Meanwhile, Rocco called Vidal for another rendezvous at the *Jean L'Amour*. The superintendent felt irritated by the sheer arrogance, but resigned himself to go with the flow. He ordered Jablonsky from the dispatcher's booth to join them at the brasserie.

"So, you're the partner; nice to meet the other half of the famous pair!" Rocco said buoyantly, shaking the major's hand.

"We met from a distance, but I guess that doesn't count—the pleasure's mine!"

"So, what brings us here on this morose afternoon?" Vidal asked impatiently.

"I know the Spaniard is in that shit hole of Fer, but I couldn't figure out where he lived—any way you could get the gendarmerie to help? Say, you could start by saying to them that your revolutionary—the guy with the scarred mug—is giving you trouble, and last you heard, he was hiding in their jurisdiction; whaddya think?"

"You mean Perez?"

"Yeah, that one!"

"Why would you want to inculpate that poor soul, he's just a megaphone artist?" Jablonsky probed.

"We're just borrowing his face, mate, nothing to it," Rocco explained.

"Of course, silly of me!" the major playacted.

"My, you guys are slow catching up!"

"Consider it done!" Vidal affirmed.

"OK, after freshening up, I'm gonna go back there. I'll call you in a couple of hours; by then, I hope you'll be able to come up with an address."

"You're talking about the gendarmerie; they do things their way," Vidal said.

"Listen, boss, you could be in Bastia or Palermo, then you'd be complaining about how long it takes for everything. I was under the assumption it was different with you, Germans," Rocco said defiantly.

"Does Jablonsky sound German to you?" the major countered, not expecting an answer.

"Maybe, you could come with me, I could use a hand?" the Sicilian wondered.

"Let's not mix apples and oranges, I have a job calling," Jablonsky returned.

"Just kidding, your partner here told me you were on surveillance duty. Maybe you can share who you're spying on when I'm done with the first mark; who knows what kind of surprise the future has in store for us!"

Ernest Jablonsky and Olive Schneider were ready. José had been briefed about what to expect; it was time to snare Rocco Giordano.

Jean-Marie Vidal received a response from the Fer gendarmerie barely a minute before the Sicilian called. The address of the presumed resident was 11 Robert Schuman Street, across from the Vogts' apartment, Stefan's old neighborhood. Rocco prided himself in having guessed right from the get-go. He parked the red Alfa at the end of the street, in the lot of the workers' quarters affectionately referred to as *the Singles*, and walked the distance to the Spaniard's hideout. The curtains were pulled. Rocco observed there was another entrance in the back of the row of apartments, accessed from the beginning of a trail that eventually lost itself in the deep forest. Kids were playing loudly, disappearing and appearing, in and out of their natural hideaways, which made the gangster unsure of his approach—he returned to the street. He then became oddly aware of his surrounding: housewives, whose lively chatting had provided a comforting background, were now looking at him, birds of prey sizing fresh road kill. The men, lubing their cars or changing sparkplugs on their mopeds, had also turned their attention to the stranger that was walking their street. At that moment, Rocco wished for the rain to send all the curious back inside. He approached Victor Vogt.

"Sorry to bother you, but I'm looking for my cousin José, I've lost his address. He has scars on his face. Any chance you can point to his door?"

"There's a new guy on the street that matches the description, but I don't recall which of the apartments he moved to," Stefan's father replied.

"You wouldn't know even if he lived across from you?" Giordano insisted.

"What kind of question is that—who the fuck do you think you are?!"

"Just answer the question, I'm not looking for a fight."

"I spoke with your man early this morning; he's from Spain. You claim to be his cousin but you dress and speak like an Italian. Last time I gave information to a stranger, my best friend was shot in the back and died at his mother's feet. Do I look like the guy who would repeat that kind of mistake? I've been around your sort before—you're nothing but fucking trouble!"

Rocco's hand twitched around the switchblade in his pocket, but he refrained from gutting the man who stood menacingly before him. Maybe after he'd be done with the Spaniard he would come back to erase his tracks. He crossed the street and knocked at the door of number 11. A tall, dark-haired, mid-aged woman opened a crack to explain she wasn't interested in buying anything today.

"Just looking for José; is he around?"

"He should be back in a while; d'you want to wait outside or inside?" she asked.

"Maybe you've got some coffee brewing; I wouldn't mind a cup?'

She closed the door behind him, just as Perez shot out of the darkness of the basement's access landing and stuck a gun to his head. Ernest Jablonsky appeared at the top of the short flight of stairs leading to the first floor, with yet another gun pointing at him. Olive Schneider, in a swift and firm maneuver, had Rocco Giordano in handcuffs before he had a chance to act.

"You said you needed my help, well, here you go! And by the way, the future surprise just tied your hands!" Jablonsky uttered, as Olive tossed her wig aside.

"You thought you could just come here and operate like you're used to in your Marseille backyard; I mean, are you guys insane or what?!" José exclaimed.

"You can't touch me—you've got nothing on me!"

"Not today, and not tomorrow either, but by Monday we'll have so much stuff on you and your brother, that you'll come to regret having ever been born," Schneider spat.

"So, you're the blonde I was gonna off?"

"Yes, what are the odds? But it looks like your plan backfired. Rest assured though, you won't have to explain your failures to Schmitt; by then he'll have more important fish to fry."

"Whatever, I'll be out of jail before you know it!"

"You're not going to jail, mister; we're not presently working for the *Police Nationale*—that would be too convenient. No, we operate from an entirely different platform, but it's not for me to say—time will tell," Olive returned with calculated disdain.

39 – FOUR & ONE (Fri)

Francis Visconti called Vidal at sixteen hours. The superintendent hadn't yet heard from Rocco and apologized for being unable to provide a lead. He hung up, somewhat frustrated by the lack of order around the mission, especially when time was of the essence. He rented a room at a seedy hotel in the Latin Quarter and decided to spend the remaining daylight in the warmth of a neighborhood café-bar with a book and a pack of *Gitanes*. Too restless to read, he instead revisited the logic of his previous thinking and reaffirmed Julia and her boyfriend had to be staying in the posh part of town. At least, it was a place to start until Rocco came up with an address. At nineteen hours, he took the métro to the Champs-Élysées and walked in the direction of the Arc de Triomphe, staying close to the crowd as he always did. He tried Vidal again, to no avail – he was on his own.

Julia, Stefan, Rémy, and Serge elected to do group shopping. They got out of the courtyard, passed the Arc de Triomphe and walked along the Champs-Élysées towards the Tuileries Garden, to catch the métro at George V. The two men were public jesters, playing their gayness to the fullest, blowing kisses to lovers, teasing those they perceived as being closet homosexuals, charming some of the ladies, but above all, shocking and enraging those less disposed to accept social divagations. Among them, a baffled Francis Visconti, who looked at the four as if he had seen ghosts, which the boys thought was hilarious.

"Did you see the face on that one!?" Rémy exclaimed.

They all laughed like small time rebels.

Visconti went on, gathering his thoughts, unable to comprehend his luck. He continued for a short length before turning around at the point he deemed appropriate for a safe distance between him and his targets. The four of them together presented an issue; he realized he might have to wait for the *faggots* to stray far enough before striking. Even better, he would follow them until they returned to their shacking grounds. It would take a lot longer, but the risk of drawing attention was minimal. It wasn't as easy as he thought to keep track of them in the crowd, especially the minute they entered the jammed subway system, with its cars often packed too tight to board. Eventually, everyone managed to hop on the same train, though Visconti had barely been able to maintain a visual on his preys. They, on the other hand, were totally unaware they had been followed by the very man they had taunted only moments ago.

Visconti almost lost the four inside a *Uniprice* supermarket in the 15th arrondissement. He had to stay farther away not to be noticed. Sometimes they would split up and take off in opposite directions, which added to the complication of not bumping into one of the pairs. Eventually, just as he thought they had slipped between his fingers, he found them waiting in line at one of the registers. He hurried out and waited across the street.

The return trip was a lot less hectic due to the reduced evening crowd. They exited the George V station, walking up the Champs Élysées, past the *Arc de Triomphe*, and onto *Avenue Foch*. Visconti followed them tightly; he was practically on them when they entered the courtyard. It was his one opportunity to strike before they would lock themselves in. Without hesitation, he raced across the cobblestones, stealthy as a leopard, pulled out his blade and leaped at Julia, counting on the element of surprise to put the others off guard just long enough to turn around and do them in one by one, while the girl bled to death on the ground. But his plan was interrupted by the bullet that left the barrel of Serge's handgun and hit him in the shoulder, sending him reeling in pain. He still tried to get to Julia, but a second shot hit him in the face, shattering his front teeth and turning his upper lip and nose to a bloody mess. He writhed in agony on the cold stone. Within minutes, the police that had been called by alarmed tenants were on the premises, quickly followed by an ambulance. In spite of the disfiguration, a policewoman identified Visconti as the man recently added to the most-wanted list by Inspector General Jacques Febrault. Serge was booked, pending verification of his category B permit. He was reassured he wasn't in trouble, considering the alternative.

Febrault was notified of the apprehension and immediately forwarded the news to all the BNFAC members. Only one hour had passed since he was made aware Rocco Giordano had also been neutralized.

Julia, Stefan, and Rémy locked themselves in, shaken by what had just happened. It was the second time in two weeks that death had come within close range of the young lovers, but things had changed; they didn't need Julia alive anymore, which made it clear someone was getting desperate. It didn't require much guessing on her part to put a face and a name on the culprit, he was no other than Chief Superintendent Joseph Pinelli, a man she had seen at the orphanage on too many occasions, and always ahead of a group of kids being taken to "Hell."

Superintendent Jean-Marie Vidal wondered why Rocco Giordano had not surfaced since he was given the Spaniard's address. He was supposed to have come up with Julia Feraez's whereabouts, to be forwarded to Francis Visconti. Something didn't add up. He called for Jablonsky, who was still technically keeping an eye on Schneider. The major responded with a positive: Olive was holed up in her house, probably sipping tisane in front of her TV set. Did Rocco walk in the Corsican's steps? Vidal called to ask the Fer gendarmerie to look into it. An hour later, the report came: the red Alfa had been found and № 11 Robert Schuman Street was vacant.

40 – NUMBER THREE (Sat)

Even though José had expressly recommended that Giuseppe di Giovanni stay in Lille, the man caught a train to Charleville-Mézière and then hopped over to Reims, in hopes of visiting the place where Clovis, unifier of the Frankish tribes, was baptized with oil from the sacred phial brought from Heaven by a dove. A city visited by popes, and the home of important archbishops, it was a place often mentioned with awe by the nuns at the orphanage, almost as fondly as Lourdes. He sensed he might never have a chance to visit the north again; it was his pilgrimage. To get close to the sacred phial kept in the Abbey of Saint-Remi was akin to touching Heaven; it was redemption—purification from sin.

Luigi Giordano knew that Di Giovanni would get lured by the history of the city. Mother Daniela's influence had made of him an extremely religious man, even if she also had taught him to err on the side of darkness. After all, it was God's will that he did the dirty work. But Luigi understood why Giuseppe had wished to distance himself from the mother superior; the cloth of his faith was made of a finer and purer thread than hers.

The yellow Alfa Romeo Giulia Sprint with the *Bouches-du-Rhône* license plates had been spotted downtown by Superintendent Alban Vasquez's men. Ernest Jablonsky had stressed that protecting Giuseppe di Giovanni was the number one priority, as the success of the BNFAC operation pivoted on critical information in his possession. No-one knew for sure if the man was actually in Reims, but Luigi seemed to think so. Vasquez had his inspectors comb all guest house registries. Sure enough, there was a man with a blind eye and burn scars registered as Marco Fini at a cheap hotel by City Hall. The bellhop said the guest had left early, enquiring about the best way to get to the Abbey of St-Remi. He also said that an Italian man with a pompadour, a golden earring, and a black leather jacket stopped by to ask the same question, half hour prior.

Vasquez was personally on it, he drove directly to the Abbey, hoping to insert himself between Giordano and Di Giovanni. But he and his men were late. Meanwhile, as he sought further information from tourists and locals, Giuseppe discovered that the *Holy Ampulla*, or what was left of it, now resided in a reliquary at the *Palace of Tau*, next to the cathedral, ironically losing both his pursuer and protector as he switched itineraries. But Giordano, who had found himself surrounded by police inside the Abbey, committed the tactical error of unsuccessfully trying to grab a stocky Irish visitor, with the intention of putting a knife to his throat. He was shot in the head by Vasquez and was pronounced dead before reaching the hospital.

The national news reported the Reims incident, but the name of the victim wasn't released, pending further investigation into the motives of the kidnapping attempt. Jean-Marie Vidal, who was left confounded and sensitized by Rocco Giordano and Francis Visconti's silence, was particularly concerned by what the newscaster had just reported. He tried to call Erik Schmitt, but there was no response. He was hardly surprised, since the Marseille superintendent was in the habit of reserving his Saturdays for socializing with the region's powers that be. At least, if the Sicilian hitmen had failed, he couldn't be put to blame, though it was going to be difficult to establish how, exactly, he had protected them, especially Rocco, who had never left the Nancy area. He called Jablonsky to ask him if he was into going out for drinks, something they were in the habit of doing. The major agreed to meet at the *Jean L'Amour*.

"By the look of it, I think Rocco Giordano could have used the help; he went missing in action after he got the address provided by the gendarmerie. Any idea what could have happened to him?"

"You put me on surveillance of Schneider, now you wonder how we could have assisted him better? Think about it for a sec."

"We either have an informant at the station or Schmitt's orders got to the Spaniard before they reached us. At any rate, since Olive was the odd man out, so to speak, I figured keeping a tab on her was the logical choice. After all, she's the one who released the Feraez girl, not to mention rumors of a blonde with a police handgun assisting the Spaniard," Vidal said.

"I thought the Corsican fabricated that story. Didn't you already discard it as nonsense?"

"I did, but then it occurred to me that Schneider hadn't been herself lately. Call it vigilance."

"On this subject, what was Muller doing patrolling the Hill Street area? Talk about subtle."

"Someone called about a suspicious character in

the neighborhood; I asked him to investigate."

"Fair enough. So, now that you need me again, are you going to share what's on your mind? I can't tell you what I think about your problems if you keep them to yourself. So, you lost Rocco; what about the others?"

"Well, problem is we lost Visconti as well, and I suspect Luigi got himself killed by the Reims police. But that could just be me being paranoid," Vidal confessed.

"I see where we might have a problem. What I don't understand is how these guys could have walked straight into a trap, if that's indeed what happened. Now you say Rocco couldn't provide Visconti with an address, so how could he have found himself in trouble? He called you, right, so we know he was waiting for information. How d'you know he didn't try to seek Schmitt's advice?"

"You have a point; maybe Rocco did the same and they've now bypassed us altogether. Perhaps it's just as well. In that case, it's possible the Spaniard has been taken care of, and Visconti is on the job in Paris, or wherever the black girl ended up staying."

"It would also mean Schmitt thinks we're useless, which has been my impression from the get-go."

"We covered up the Toul fiasco; that's not exactly nothing, is it?"

"Touché! At any rate, I trust it should all become clear by Monday," Jablonsky contended.

41 – BEFORE THE STORM (Sun)

Julia was crying in Stefan arms. He wasn't doing that much better, trying his best to hold off the tears, feeling he needed to stay strong to provide support. Rémy was a mess, talking too fast in a high-pitched voice, showing his shaking hand around as if to prove he was having a nervous breakdown. They were all due to show up at the station on Monday for a deposition, which paused problems for all of them. Somehow, and because of the chaos that ensued from the attack, the policewoman who had identified Francis Visconti had not asked for IDs; she just took names, addresses, and phone numbers.

Serge had returned from the station in the early morning and went straight to sleep. He was alright; just a bit shaken by the event, but glad he was able to save a life beside his own – possibly, he had saved them all.

There was a knock at the door. Julia opened it after looking through the bird's eye viewer. The man in the suit told the two officers that had accompanied him, to wait in the black DS 21 parked in the courtyard.

"I'm Controller General Jacques Febrault of the city police. The reason for my visit is to inform you that you don't have to show up at the precinct tomorrow. In other words, you're off the hook. But I'm here in a different capacity altogether. I don't know much about you, Rémy, except that I recommend you find a much less dangerous profession; but I am quite familiar with you, Miss Feraez, and young Stefan here, for having read the files put together by Commandant Olive Schneider. I understand you are minors, but I have been made aware that you are in the custody of much respected individuals, and that's good enough for me. I am not at liberty to tell what our plans are, but you will be required, at some future point, to testify before judges of the High Court. I count on you, especially you, Miss Feraez, to make yourself available. So, don't run away until that happens; can I trust you on that?"

"As long as you promise these assassins will stop showing up, I have no need to hide. As a matter of fact, I've been waiting to tell my story for a long time—you can count on me, Sir."

"You too, Stefan, you will need to testify for what happened in Toul a couple of weeks ago, as well as here yesterday. And of course, Rémy, you will have a chance to tell your version of the event. I shall keep you posted. By the way, Julia, Commandant Schneider asked me to tell you that she might have something for you soon regarding personal matters. She will contact you. Other duties are calling—you all have a restful day."

Jacques Febrault's steps were heard down the stairs and across the courtyard, then the purr of the Citroën's engine gently faded away.

Superintendent Vasquez eventually caught up with Giuseppe di Giovanni. He advised him to either stay in Reims or go to Paris, where he would also be put under police protection. The Sicilian chose to remain close to the *Holy Ampulla* and the magnificent *Notre-Dame de Reims* cathedral, where he could spend his days praying. He had already made up his mind of joining a monastery if he ever survived Schmitt's men, even if it meant sweeping cold stones and trimming hedges for the rest of his life. He was also prepared to uncover Mother Daniela's wrongdoings, and the countless men and women that were behind the horrendous psychological and physical abuse suffered by the children who passed through the orphanage. He had their names, places, statuses. Since Jesus spoke to him, he had recorded everything into a log kept in a luggage locker at the Toulon train station, away from Schmitt and Pinelli's scrutiny.

Vidal finally spoke with Schmitt, who assured him he hadn't been bypassed. Rather, his men were used to working alone. Most likely, the Giordanos had entered in communication with Visconti and all was under control. All he needed to preoccupy himself with was protection and cleanup. The mess couldn't make the news, period.

"How's Olive doing, still being a good girl?"

"Well, she claimed to be sick and had to take off. But she's been worrying me, so I put Ernest on her to make sure she was staying home." Vidal replied.

"What, you think she's the blonde with the gun the Corsican was mumbling about?"

"You never know."

"Correct, but you made sure to put someone on Jablonsky as well, like I taught you, right?"

"Yes, I got one of my best patrol guys to make sure he wasn't goofing off."

"So, you suspect Jablonsky too?"

"Well, he's my right hand man; I have to trust him, but I'm not sure he agrees with me on Schneider."

"So, you're saying you wanted to make sure

Ernest stayed on Olive?"

"Correct, as far as I know, he did."

"And you trust Muller to not take the opportunity to hit the shooting range instead?"

"It's always a possibility, but I'm sure he must be aware of the heavy consequences of not following orders; I've got to trust him not to be that stupid."

"Perhaps, but who else could wage for him sticking to the job?"

"It sounds like you don't trust Muller, or even Jablonsky," Vidal said.

"I'm just tapping into your own distrust. Me, I'm in fucking Marseille; what do I know about your operation beside what you tell me?"

"I guess, I've always been an open book to you, but you're right, I'm concerned about the Spaniard always being a step ahead of us. You're sure you don't have leaks at your end?"

"First of all, since you mentioned books, the teacher's first job is to open the book that is the student. He must see him naked before he even considers handing down his knowledge to him. He knows when that student jacks off with one hand while sticking a finger up his ass with the other. He knows his truths and his lies. So no, Jean-Marie, you can't hide from me. That being said, don't ever fucking doubt the tightness of my operation; if there're leaks, you own the damned colander!"

"If you're saying I've got a traitor at the highest level; that only leaves Schneider or Jablonsky."

"Or both, or your entire fucking department! Are you sure you're not the one being played?"

"As far as I know I'm still the captain of my ship."

"In that case, why should you concern yourself

with what Schneider does in the privacy of her home; she's just a secretary for Christ's sake! You're wasting precious resources by putting Jablonsky on surveillance when he could be assisting Rocco in dealing with the Spaniard and his accomplices. Call me tomorrow when you have some real news; and do me a favor, get a fucking spine!" Schmitt uttered, having ran out of patience for his protégé.

Toulon's Chief Superintendent Jean-Marc Poitier and five of the BNFAC members, including Controller General Paul Mattaf, Superintendents Claude Henry and Jules Broussard, plus the two Paris commandants had gathered in preparation of the arrests of Erik Schmitt and Joseph Pinelli. Poitier, who was familiar with the floor plan of the Marseille station, had explained how to simultaneously surprise both men with warrants. The local gendarmerie had been alerted and was ready to intervene in case of resistance. Other officers in the Marseille force had also been targeted as the result of Corinne Jones' investigation forwarded to Jacques Febrault in Paris, and from which warrants were issued.

Later that day, the other half of the BNFAC met at Frederic Jung's office in Metz to go over the final details of Vidal's apprehension and the logistics of putting Rocco Giordano behind bars. The gangster had been locked with a portable potty in an old concrete blockhouse inside a decommissioned army base, twenty-five kilometers outside Nancy. Lance Merckx was in charge of keeping an eye on him; both the FBN and the BNFAC needed him healthy. Vidal's arrest had been set at half-past eight, the time at which he regularly came into his office. Ernest Jablonsky and Olive Schneider would be there first to give the signal to the four superintendents waiting outside. The clock was in countdown mode.

42 – THE ARREST (Mon)

Jean-Marc Poitier, Paul Mattaf, and one of the commandants entered Ernest Pinelli's office, disregarding his secretary's objections. The three flashed their new badges, while they read him his rights, which were few.

"What the fuck is the BNFAC?" the chief superintendent asked defensively.

"It stands for the highest echelon of the *Police Nationale* sick and tired of criminals in its ranks delegitimizing its work; that's it in a nutshell. Don't tell me you didn't see it coming!" Poitier snapped.

"Are you guys idiots or what; what kind of process is this?!"

"The process you refer to is called your arrest. We advise you to not resist," Controller General Paul Mattaf warned.

"Well, I'm resisting!"

Poitier called the gendarmerie squadron leader stationed outside the building.

"Time to come in," he just said.

Meanwhile, the other three BNFAC agents in charge of apprehending Erik Schmitt were also having a hard time convincing the superintendent to surrender.

"Go fuck yourself!" he spat before calling for enforcement.

"Your personnel are now officially operating under our authority; the majority of your officers and their men are complying and assisting us in rounding up those we have warrants for," Superintendent Jules Broussard said sternly.

Schmitt pulled a revolver from his desk drawer.

"This joke has lasted long enough, you three get out of here pronto or I start shooting!"

Four squadron men with assault rifles ran in through the left-open office door, pointing their guns at the superintendent.

"Put your weapon down, now!" an order shot.

Schmitt fired, hitting one of the gendarmes in the arm. The only thing that prevented a rain of bullets from downing the beleaguered officer, was a pressing order from Febrault that he was to be taken alive at all cost. Superintendent Broussard, who had come from behind in a flash, subdued him with a hit to the back of the head. Schmitt was pinned to the floor and put in handcuffs, before being dragged out of his office. By then, the station had been overtaken by gendarmerie forces.

Following protocol, the highest uncompromised ranking officers were instated as provisional chief superintendent and superintendent to replace Pinelli and Schmitt. The local papers had also been summoned to cover the arrests. The BNFAC had sent their first warning.

When Vidal entered his office, he was surprised to find both Jablonsky and Schneider at their posts. Normally, the major didn't come in till the beginning of his standard shift at ten, while Olive started at nine.

"What brings you two in ahead of schedule?"

227

"Actually, we have a lot on our plates today, so we thought we'd get an early start," Ernest answered.

"Something happened I should know about?"

"Well, we're expecting a few guests from out of town; kind of a surprise," Schneider said.

"Why wasn't I told?"

"It will soon make plenty of sense, Jean-Marie," Jablonsky replied.

"Cut the crap, will you, I'm not into riddles this morning!"

"Alright then, ever heard of the BNFAC...? Me neither until about a week ago; it stands for the *National Bureau of Anti-Corruption Forces*. It's a special branch headed by Inspector General Jacques Febrault of the *Police Nationale*, and to which both Olive and I belong. Is it starting to ring a bell?" Jablonsky explained.

"I have no idea what you're talking about!"

"Remember the blonde with the P1 working with the Spaniard? Allow me to introduce Commandant Schneider! The Spaniard is indeed José Perez, agent for the FBN—I'm sure the name is familiar. As to me, I have been a liaison for the U.S. agency long enough to know all the villains protecting the drug route and other traffics in this area," the major continued.

Vidal was livid—a mix of rage and fright. It made sense all at once.

"In about a minute, our four guests will walk in this office and recite you your rights; then they'll take you to Charles III prison, pending your transfer to the appropriate location. So that you should know, Rocco Giordano is presently on his way to a maximum security facility, his brother Luigi was shot dead in Reims by one of our imminent visitors, and Francis Visconti is in a Paris hospital going through reconstructive surgery after his face was blown off. It also means that Julia Feraez and Stefan Vogt are alive and well. Now, say hello to our guests!" Olive Schneider said.

Frederic Jung came in first.

"I never understood why you were so enamored with Erik Schmitt. For your information, I just heard he had to be subdued after firing a gun at the squad forces of the gendarmerie—not exactly the work of wisdom... Jean-Marie Vidal, you are under arrest!"

Superintendents Alban Vasquez, Marcel Paroie, and George Stiegler followed in, each taking turns explaining the nature of their presence. Vidal didn't resist. He stood a broken man, silent tears running down his ashen cheeks; obscure goals driven by untethered ambitions shattered like the crystal of an incandescent bulb hitting the concrete floor. He was the empty shell of an experiment gone wrong at the shared hand of greed and hubris. Olive Schneider felt sorry for him. Ernest Jablonsky looked at him one last time in the eyes.

"It's not like I didn't warn you all these years," he said, as Vidal was handcuffed and taken away.

43 – CONSEQUENCES

Within days, thirty two high-ranking officers of the *Police Nationale* were arrested under various warrants issued by the BNFAC. As more men and women confessed, the effect became akin to the avalanche that followed the snowball, reaching all levels of the social makeup, including politics, businesses, social agencies, and even the military. But while the issue of corruption within the system was the focus of the BNFAC, Corinne Jones and Lance Merckx were busy consolidating years of investigative work around the Corsican clans and the various Sicilian families accused of trading with Turkey and running the Marseille clandestine labs, with the purpose of turning over the results to the French authorities.

José and Olive Schneider, with the help of Julia and Giuseppe di Giovanni, were channeling their efforts into cataloging the names of those involved in the trade of orphans, as well as the ones responsible for the disappearance of runaways and parentless juvenile emigrants. All the cases overlapped in some form or another, mostly in the shape of the same faces surfacing across the many branches of criminality that laundered enormous amount of money via fake fronts, while bribing and manipulating those whose moral compasses had long lost their pointers. Joseph Pinelli was found guilty of running a ring of child pornography and prostitution, whose *supplies* came directly from Mother Daniela Graziano's *select product line*, known in private circles as the Hell Children. Additionally, the head nun, in cahoots with the mafia and some CPS agents, arranged direct sales with clients whose intentions rarely were to benefit the children. For instance, Julia was merely a sex toy gifted to the adolescent boys of the family whose parents deemed their offspring eligible for hands-on education. Rape often led to beatings, and for some unfortunate souls, beatings to monstrous injuries, and eventually death, naturally followed by a demand for fresh supplies. The orphanage and the CPS made sure the survivors had *never* visited those families, as files were tampered with or lost, and the victims were made to "forget," generally requiring "appropriate" psychiatric treatment by complicit doctors, or clinics willing to look the other way in exchange for funding. The basic reality of it, as José saw it, was that *dirty wealth* always ended up feeding the utmost depraved and abject side of bankrupt morality.

Shortly before Mother Daniela Graziano's mysterious disappearance, Giuseppe di Giovanni paid the nun a visit. He had arrived with Olive Schneider and Julia Feraez, who remained in the waiting room until the time would come to call them in.

"I was wondering if you would ever visit again, my son. I overheard you stayed in Bastia after you left without a word. But God forgives, for I rest assured you came here for forgiveness," she said acidly.

"I actually came to you to say goodbye, because I am very certain you and I will never see each other again. As to forgiveness, what is there to forgive? I served you because I was convinced I was serving the Blessed Virgin. But one night, after awakening from the heinousness of my crimes, her son, Jesus, appeared before me. He told me that the path to redemption was beyond these walls, outside in the world where the children needed my help. 'Go and save them!' he said. And so, I did. That's why I left you, but I never abandoned the orphans."

"The Blessed Virgin speaks through me; I am her voice and her orders are to never be challenged—they are God's order! You, on the other hand, are a servant bound to obedience, to the execution of these orders; any deviance from them is the work of Satan! The voices you hear are nothing but your own guilt taunting you for not serving the Holy Virgin."

"I don't possess the will to counter your corrupt logic, but you must be aware by now that Schmitt and Pinelli have been arrested. Your name has been repeatedly showing up in depositions. The French authorities have contacted the Vatican about your involvement with sending the mafia after Julia Feraez, as well as your activities around the traffic of orphans, those your version of the Blessed Virgin ordered me to drive to pornographic photo shoots and rape families. You looked the other way when your right hand, Sister Henrietta, molested and tortured children. I was one of them, remember? And so was Julia Feraez, who ran in fear and indescribable pain the night I hit the nun in the head with the fire poker and inserted the crucifix in her entrails. You wanted Julia to make her pay for her crimes before having her killed for what she knew, but she didn't do it, you see; I'm the one who gave Henrietta what she deserved. I could have killed her—maybe I should have—but I remembered my list of mortal sins— what I had done was bad enough! On the other hand, I don't think the nun was going to stop beating Julia until she was dead; why I intervened. Now, there are two people in the waiting room, one you will recognize and who would also like to say goodbye; the other—anxious to meet you—Commandant Olive Schneider of the *Police Nationale*, a woman who has been intrigued by irregularities in orphanages and CPS since she and her husband adopted in the mid fifties."

Giuseppe opened the door to let them in. Julia walked straight to the head nun.

"I was hoping to never see you again, but your relentless wish to have me brought back here has made me curious. What exactly did you and Henrietta intend on doing with me? Please, feel free to share with the Commandant," she said venomously.

The nun looked at her with coal eyes.

"Go burn in Hell!"

"I already have—you run the place!"

The next day, a black Mercedes Benz 600 took Daniela Graziano and Henrietta Mazzoti to an undisclosed location. It was rumored the Vatican had a version of Hell specifically tailored for those who had "unintentionally" blemished the name of God. It was one of the rare instances of the French authorities looking the other way, and one during which Chief Superintendent Jean-Marc Poitier, of Toulon, made sure to be busy. For those who would later be looking for the two nuns, they were never heard of, for none of the original sisters remained at the orphanage—no traces were left. Well, not completely, since Giuseppe di Giovanni reassumed his post as groundkeeper and general maintenance manager.

Except that he would no longer be driving children to Ernest Pinelli's playhouses, or delivering to rape families.

Before driving to the Marseille orphanage, Olive was able to contact the Hayeses in Oakland to ascertain Ben was indeed Amadi, Julia's long estranged brother. José had swung by the Paris studio to inform the teens that they were no longer in harm's way. A few days later, Schneider arrived with the news. Julia was stunned, as if surprise and relief couldn't find a place to settle in the same emotional compartment. Then, all at once, she jumped up, squealing with joy, to hug the officer.

Stefan remained the observer, as he had been all along. His story was too short and inconsequential compared to what others his age had already gone through or accomplished. Yet, his escape from his psychological enclave had triggered a set of probabilities that afforded the forces of justice to come forward at exactly the right time. He was rejoiced for Julia, who now had the perfect excuse to visit her chosen city. He understood that soon enough, the two would go different ways. Perhaps, one day, when he and his rock and roll band would tour the States, they might bump into each other again, and who knows what would happen then? But they still had a couple of months living and exploring together. Two months was a long time in teen years.

44 – LATER

The BNFAC was reabsorbed by the *Police Nationale*, ending Jacques Febrault's dream of turning it into a powerful agency or ministry. But a myth was born around *the Incorruptibles* that would never leave the psyche of the force. Eventually, what would become the French Connection was defeated because of it.

Olive Schneider became Chief Superintendent for Nancy, with promoted Superintendent Ernest Jablonsky as her right hand. George Muller and half a dozen minor offenders at the station were terminated from their posts.

When *the office* closed, Corinne, Lance, José, Olive, and Ernest went out for drinks to toast a job well done and wish luck to the next generation of vigilantes. The FBN was no longer. Lance would return to Holland and Corinne was torn between France and the States. José and his wife, Lizzy, had no plans to leave Nancy, they loved it there and the safe houses still needed them until one day, and in a better world, the state would take over.

Stefan stayed in Paris until he turned eighteen. He never saw Victor again. Inevitably, and with much practice, he became good at the guitar, joining progressive recording bands and playing the *Bataclan* regularly alongside Gong, Triangle, Ange, Magma, Zoo, Marin Circus, Au Bonheur des Dames, etc... He moved to Britain following his army time in Germany, to further hone his musical skills and own his right of passage into the world of Anglo-American rock, a family he had dreamt of joining since he heard John Lennon sing "Ain't She Sweet" way back when.

He and Julia eventually reconnected with each other in San Francisco. They slept a few times together, intent on rekindling the passions of the early days; but things had changed, as inexplicable forces pulled them in different directions. But what hadn't changed was the immutable place they had for each other in their hearts. There was never a day that would pass without a thought, a face that appeared in the mirror of the soul, a moment of yearning for something that only lived behind the veil of time. They looked at each other from across a window that existed nowhere else, smiling, acknowledging, acceptant of what they had received and surrendered.

Love is eternal.

END

NAME INDEX

Monique Colbert: CPS case manager, Marseille, suspect
Mario Oliveira: CPS case manager, Marseille
Joseph Pinelli: chief superintendent, Marseille,
     prime suspect
Mother Daniela Graziano: head nun, Marseille,
     prime suspect
Sister Henrietta Mazzoti: nun, abuser, crime victim,
     suspect
Gaston Deferre: mayor of Marseille (real public figure,
     mentioned in passing)
Sergio, aka the Corsican: hitman hired by E. Schmitt
Emile Dollinger: Nancy cab driver
Corinne Jones: associate of *the office*, FBN agent,
     aka Evelyn Chabron
Giuseppe di Giovanni: Sicilian mafia, later French
     Connection, informer
Marco Fini: also Giuseppe di Giovanni
Lance Merckx: associate of *the office*, FBN agent,
     Rotterdam liaison
Luigi Giordano: Sicilian mafia, Rocco's brother
Rocco Giordano: Sicilian mafia, Luigi's brother
Alban Desfrères: friend of José's, driver
Martine & Sylvie: Paris prostitutes
Rémy & Serge: Paris gay male prostitutes
Alain: owner of the Paris studios
Frederic Jung: superintendent, Metz, BNFAC
George Stiegler: superintendent, Mulhouse, BNFAC
Marcel Paroie: superintendent, Dijon, BNFAC
Alban Vasquez: superintendent, Reims, BNFAC
Jean-Marc Poitier: chief superintendent, Toulon, BNFAC
Jacques Febrault: inspector general of the *Police
     Nationale*, BNFAC
Paul Mattaf: controller general, BNFAC

Claude Henry: superintendent, Limoges, BNFAC
Jules Broussard: superintendent, Orleans, BNFAC
James Nichols: FBN agent, Marseille
Evelyn Chabron: aka Corinne Jones
Ben Hayes: also Amadi Feraez
Alexander & Aurora Hayes: Ben Hayes' parents
     (see Amadi Feraez)

Stups: French for narcs
BNFAC: *Bureau National des Forces Anti-Corruption*
     (National Bureau of Anti-Corruption Forces)
FBN: Federal Bureau of Narcotics
BNDD: Bureau of Narcotics and Dangerous Drugs
CPS: Child Protection Services
SDECE: *Service de Documentation Exterieure et de*
     Contre-Espionage (External Documentation &
     Counter-Espionage Service) France's external
     intelligence agency from 1944 to 1982
DST: *Direction de la Surveillance du Territoire*
     (Directorate of Territorial Surveillance) French
     intelligence agency, branch of the *Police*
     Nationale

OTHER WORKS
BY THE AUTHOR

The Disappearance of Olaf Swyndle (An Improbable Emergence – book 1)

The Hektor Dilemma (A.I.E. – book 2)

Ma-l's Grand Gathering (A.I.E. – book 3)

Convergence of the Realms (A.I.E. – book 4)

Reyes & Leeds

Story of a Tale-Maker

Nine Amber Pieces

A Life Given, a Life Taken

francisvoignier.com
Dolosse & Writs, Eureka, California